CHARM HIS PANTS OFF

A WITCHES THREE COZY MYSTERY

CATE MARTIN

Cover design by Shezaad Sudar.

Ratatoskr Press logo by Aidan Vincent.

ISBN 978-1-946552-97-6

❀ Created with Vellum

FREE EBOOK!

Like exclusive, free content?

If you'd like to receive "Enter Three Witches" a free trilogy of short stories, a prequel to the Witches Three Cozy Mystery series, go to CateMartin.com to subscribe to my monthly newsletter! This eBook is exclusively for newsletter subscribers and will never be sold in stores. Check it out!

CHAPTER 1

ost people when they think of winter imagine a Christmas scene, or perhaps something related to New Year's Eve: people gathered in warmth and light, the cold dark kept safely on the other side of frosted windows. But to me, that's not really winter. That's just the first tease of what's to come.

And this had been a very fine winter so far. Lots of snow, but when it hadn't been snowing the sky had been clear and blue, the sun shining brightly if with little heat. I love snow and ice and every activity that involves them, but even I can feel my mood lifted when constantly bathed in sunlight.

Not that I had much time for winter sports. No, it wasn't skiing or skating or snowboarding keeping me out in the cold sun every morning.

It was the time portal. The three of us could do magic from anywhere, but for the delicate spells that kept the protective wards on the time portal strong, it was better to be just at the spot in the orchard where 2019 met the bridge back to 1928.

The three of us were out there for hours every morning. We hadn't seen a single sign of anyone trying to get across or even just probe our wards in search of weaknesses, but we had all agreed it was best to err on the side of caution.

So each day just after dawn we'd meet out in the frozen orchard under the glistening, icicle-laden boughs of the fruit treesg to work magic together. We never spoke a word until we were done, but we no longer needed to use our voices to communicate. We sensed each other's intentions as we passed the magical energy between us. It was not quite reading each other's minds, but it was scarily close.

On that particular morning, I was certain the other two were tuning out the soreness I was feeling all over my body. I had added weight to nearly every lift when working out the day before. It had felt great yesterday, and it was awesome to get back into a weightlifting regime after so many years of missed workouts.

But when I woke up, I had felt like I'd been trampled by a herd of angry bulls. I had tried to do a little yoga before coming out to the yard, but my arms and legs were still trembling as we worked the spell, and I could see Brianna and Sophie out of the corners of my eyes. Their up-raised arms were trembling too.

At least Sophie had found a warmer parka and wool pants, so she was no longer setting us all shivering in sympathy to the cold air biting deep into her Southern bones.

I don't know how to explain what we were doing since there was nothing we were seeing, but we all three felt a ball of energy moving around, sometimes in the center of our little circle and sometimes moving from one to the other of us. We didn't direct it; it just knew where all three of us wanted it to go. It was strange, that feeling of controlling it but also of having no control.

Sophie made a spinning motion with her arms as if she had that ball close to her chest and was wrapping it in protective warmth. Then she floated it over to me, and as so often happened when Sophie's magic touched me, I smelled jasmine and rich coffee, and a rush of warmth filled me.

That was nice, that warmth. It loosened my muscles just a bit, took the edge off the aching soreness.

I also got a glimpse of what Sophie had seen, the way she used magic to sense things, and particularly to sense the time portal and the wards. I brought that sense with me like a hand-drawn map as I sunk deep into my own perceptions of the world as a web of bright threads. My mind raced over the network of connections.

As always, I sensed the presence of Juno, or benefactor's sister, caught up in the web of threads that was the bridge. But, as always, she didn't answer my call. Why did she hide, only emerging at the most inopportune of moments? Why couldn't we speak to her when the world was calm and actual conversations would be possible?

I felt the energy flow away from me, and I concentrated my mind on making a last snapshot of the thread world before that flow passed from me to Brianna.

Brianna's fingers danced as if she were playing an instrument or typing on a computer at lightning speed. She was so full of magic her hair was floating up behind her like Superman's cape, snapping with more than mere static electricity. I felt the hairs on the back of my own neck start to lift as well, a tickly sensation.

Then suddenly my mind was full of chatter, random words that eluded my efforts to string them together. It was like a hundred half-formed thoughts all overlapping.

I didn't realize we had all been floating until we all fell at once, slipping on the icy snow to land on our backsides, hair spilling down in a perfectly ordinary way.

"What was that?" Sophie asked, pressing her mittened hand to her forehead.

"Did something just try to communicate with us?" I asked. "Something... alien?"

"Sorry," Brianna said, her cheeked flushed red, not from the cold. "Sorry. I tried to hold it back."

"Hold what back?" I asked.

"My thoughts," she said. "Oh, how embarrassing to lose control like that. I completely lost my still pond."

"Your still pond?" Sophie asked.

"That's the image I use to quiet my mind for magical work," Brianna said, still blushing furiously.

"Those were your thoughts?" I asked. She nodded. "I couldn't catch a single one of them."

"Me neither," Sophie said. "Is it always like that in your head?"

"No," Brianna said, but the way she wouldn't meet our eyes made me doubt she was being entirely honest. She added, so softly we could barely hear the words, "I can follow it all."

"Well, all of the protections on the time portal looked in order to me," I said, getting up and brushing the snow from my backside.

"Me too," Sophie said, accepting my hand up.

"And here I was worried I was distracting the two of you with my exhausted muscles."

"I think body information is easier to tune out than mind information," Sophie said, but she was rolling her shoulders in a way that looked like it would work out the kink I had there. I don't think she knew she was doing it.

"That's probably true," Brianna said. "I try to keep my filters up for just that reason. But the picture of the thread world that moved from Amanda to me was just so much clearer than ever before; it was overwhelming. It gave me so many ideas of things I want to explore and research and test."

"I've been getting a clearer picture too," Sophie said. "We've made a lot of progress so far this year."

"But there's so much further to go," Brianna said. "If only we knew what we were up against."

"Twelve plus Evanora," I said. "That's what Otto said."

"But is that twelve witches?" Brianna asked. "Maybe they're not all witches. The coven back in Boston only had a couple of real witches in it."

"For that matter, there could be more than twelve too," Sophie said. "Amanda didn't know how many she was sensing surrounding her at the New Year's Eve party."

"Until we go back, we can't know for sure," I said.

"And we're not ready to go back," Brianna said. "Not yet."

We'd been having various versions of this conversation for six weeks now.

"Let's go in," Sophie said, thrusting her mittened hands into the pockets of her parka and hunching down inside its collar. "Lunch will warm us up."

Brianna and I nodded, and the three of us tromped across the snow to the back door.

"I just feel like they're waiting for us, just on the other side of the bridge," Brianna said.

"None of us have sensed that," I said.

"No, but all the same. I feel like they are. They're waiting for us to make the first move," she said.

"Or we hope they are," Sophie said as she pulled open the door and we quickly passed into the solarium, shutting the door before shedding our layers of outdoor clothing. "They could be doing anything back in 1928. How would we know?"

"Anything big would have a historical effect," Brianna said.

"There's a lot of nonhistorical level stuff they could do that could harm us," Sophie said.

"Let's not get too worried about hypotheticals," I said. "Especially not when Mr. Trevor made us something that smells absolutely divine. Is that pumpkin soup?"

"Indeed it is," he said as we came into the kitchen. He had heard us come in and was already filling bowls and setting them on the kitchen table where a basket of bread rolls and a dish of butter were waiting.

"Hot soup," Sophie said, sliding into her chair. I swear she had a spoonful in her mouth before she'd even settled onto her seat. "Warm perfection."

"I'm glad you like it," Mr. Trevor said. "Any plans for the day?"

"Just the usual," I said as I buttered a roll. "Brianna will be hitting the library to follow up on that barrage of thoughts that she just washed over Sophie and me with. I have another cleansing ritual to do with my wand down in the cellar; hopefully, this one will do the trick but who knows. Sophie?"

"Wand work for me too," she said. "I promise not to set the floorboards on fire again."

"That is, of course, appreciated," Mr. Trevor said. "But what I was actually inquiring about was this evening. Will we all be eating together, or were any of you going out?"

We all looked at each other and shook our heads.

"Why do you ask?" Sophie asked. Mr. Trevor generally just left food out for each of us to eat whenever we were hungry. "Were you going out? Because we can totally fend for ourselves. You spoil us, you know."

"No, I had no plans," Mr. Trevor said. "I was just planning a special dessert. Chocolate lava cakes. But they are best eaten when they're still warm, so we should plan to all sit down together."

"That sounds amazing," Sophie said.

"But why the special dessert?" I asked.

Mr. Trevor looked at me like he thought I was joking. Then he looked at Brianna, who had stopped listening to the conversation a few moments ago and was scribbling in her notebook, and finally Sophie, who looked as curious as I was.

"Well, it's Valentine's Day," he said. "None of you had plans?"

"Not this year," Sophie said glumly, drawing swirls in the bottom of her soup bowl with her spoon.

"No, not me," I said. I had on occasion seen Nick jog past the charm school, his grandfather's Irish setter Finnegan trotting beside him, but we hadn't spoken yet that year. I had occasionally felt the urge to run out and bump into him, but I had no idea what I'd say. The fact that I was a witch would always be a wall between us now that he knew, whether or not I was actively messing in his world of police work by investigating some crime that crossed the time portal or not.

Mr. Trevor looked at Brianna scribbling away until she sensed him waiting for her to speak.

"No plans," she said. "Just research in the library with my cats."

The trio of stray cats that Brianna had adopted at Christmas had the run of the entire house, but much like Brianna they mainly stayed in the library. She loved them to bits but hadn't seen the point in giving them actual names. Sophie and I had finally been compelled to name them ourselves. The black cat with the white spot under his chin was Jones, the ginger one with the crook in his tail was Ziggy, and the white one with one green eye and one blue eye was Duke.

"I hope it's not a sensitive topic," Mr. Trevor said.

"Not at all," I said, and Sophie gave him a smile that almost looked genuine.

"We have a deeper calling," she said. "And there's no one I'd rather spend any holiday at all with than my housemates."

"Splendid," Mr. Trevor said, clapping his hands together. "Than shall we gather in the dining room this evening at six o'clock?"

"Sounds great," I said. Sophie nodded. Mr. Trevor glanced at Brianna. "I'll make sure she's there on time," I promised.

"Thank you," he said, then left the kitchen, his footsteps echoing up the back stairs to his personal office.

"You still haven't talked to Nick," Sophie said.

"No," I said. "But what about you?"

"Me?" Sophie said. "I've not met a single person since I moved here. Not in the present, anyway."

"I know," I said. "I just meant, the way you said you had no plans this year. It kind of sounded like other years you did."

"I did," Sophie said, getting up to take her bowl to the sink and rinse it out before putting it in the dishwasher. She dried her hands on a towel, but I could tell she felt my eyes still on her. "That was back in New Orleans."

"Maybe there's a way you can take a break and get away-" I started to say, but Sophie shook her head.

"No," she said. "Everything nearly fell apart when you left last fall."

"Brianna and I are both stronger now," I said, and Brianna looked up, confused, upon hearing her name.

"Yes, but back then we didn't even have an enemy to guard against," Sophie said.

"Not that we knew of," I said.

"No, I can't go," Sophie said. "Not now, and perhaps not ever. That's the commitment we all made to Miss Zenobia. I won't go back on my word."

I looked to Brianna for backup, but she just gave me a sad little

7

shake of her head. "Sophie's right. For all we know, Evanora and her cohorts will know if any of us leave. They might be waiting for just that opportunity."

"All the more reason to call them out," I said.

"Not yet," Sophie said. Brianna's hand touched my arm, and I realized my own hands had balled into tight fists. I was always too eager to get the fight over with.

"I hate waiting," I grumbled, but forced my body to relax.

"We're not waiting," Sophie said, taking the two remaining bowls off the table and bringing them to the sink. "We're preparing."

"But at some point, we're as prepared as well can be," I said. "Will we know when we reach that point?"

"We will," Brianna said. "We'll know."

I was doubtful, but there was no point in arguing about it all afternoon. Even if it was a nice excuse to procrastinate on checking on my wand. My traitorous, spying wand.

We were just giving each other little nods of farewell, me to head to the solarium and get back into my coat and boots to head down to the cellar, Brianna and Sophie to head up to the library and attic respectively, when we all froze in place at the sound of a knock on the door.

A perfectly mundane knock at the door, and yet a tingle of fear was dancing up my spine. And Brianna and Sophie were similarly struck, eyes wide, none of us moving.

"It could be a package or something," I said. But we never got packages.

"Well, there's one way to find out," Sophie said and headed down the long corridor to the front door.

For a moment I was convinced it would be Nick standing there, perhaps with a single rose in his outstretched hand, showing up completely out of the blue just because it was Valentine's Day.

Ugh. Sometimes my brain can be so stupid. There was no hope of that. Summoning up the image just made me feel worse than before.

So it was a little startling when the first thing I glimpsed as the door swung open was indeed a single red rose. But the man holding it wasn't Nick. It was no one I recognized.

No, this was an attractive young black man about our age. And judging from his clothing, he wasn't a local. He was dressed far too lightly for the weather, his jacket little more than a windbreaker, his boots totally inadequate for more than a light rain. His head was half shaved, half tightly breaded cornrows swept up into a topknot that looked sleekly dignified but in no way kept his ears warm.

He stood there smiling warmly at Sophie, waiting for her to say something first or to take the flower he was still holding out for her.

But finally the cold defeated him, and he decided to make the next move. "Hello, Sophie," he said. "Long time no see."

Sophie said nothing at all. She just let her hand drop away from the door, and the door swung back shut right in that man's startled face.

CHAPTER 2

For a moment, it was as if the closing of the door put us all under some sort of freezing spell. Brianna and I stood dumbstruck in the back of the foyer, staring at the motionless silhouette of Sophie standing with her nose mere inches from the heavy wood door. None of us spoke, and the strange young man didn't knock again.

Finally, I found my voice, although it squeaked out the first word. "Sophie?" I called. "Is everything all right?" She didn't answer me. I cleared my throat and tried again. "Are you sensing danger?"

"Danger," Brianna said, and suddenly her wand was in her hand, the tip glowing like a bright ember, casting her face in an orange light that danced through the strands of her red hair.

Sophie turned to look back at us and raised a single hand, motioning for Brianna to lower her wand.

"Do you think the coven sent him?" Brianna asked, lowering her wand but not putting it away.

"No, this has nothing to do with the coven," Sophie said. Then she took a big, shaky breath and squared her shoulders. "I've got this."

"We've got your back," I said, and Brianna nodded.

Sophie gave us a smile only lightly touched by the sardonic part of her personality. Then she turned her attention back to the front porch as she opened the door.

The young man was still standing there. He was even still smiling, although there was a confused look to his eyes as if he wasn't sure if Sophie were teasing him or not.

"It's kind of cold out here, Sophie," he said.

"Yes, sorry. Please come in," she said. Belatedly she realized she was still blocking his way and stepped back to let him past her.

"What's in the box?" Brianna demanded. Her wand was out of sight, but she was still on the lookout for danger.

"Oh, Brianna, right?" he said. "And you must be Amanda," he said, turning his warm brown gaze to me. "I brought treats. Beignets. From Auntie Claire," he added, his eyes now on Sophie. Sophie took the box from him numbly.

"Is that a bakery in New Orleans?" I asked. He only had the lightest of accents, like Sophie's it was hard to place it as actually southern and not just some sort of cosmopolitan thing.

"No, no," he said with a wide smile. "Auntie Claire is my auntie. Sophie knows her."

"She makes the best beignets in New Orleans," Sophie said. Her accent was stronger than usual. I wondered if this was homesickness, an unconscious response to the guy's familiar accent, or something else.

I knew from experience that Sophie adjusted her accent to suit her needs, laying it on thick when she wanted a layer between her and other people. But surely that was just for strangers? Not for this young man who shared a linguistic origin with her?

"I'll heat these up," Sophie said, then headed down the corridor with the takeout box. The young man seemed uncertain if he should follow her or not. After a moment he decided the correct thing to do was to take off his wet boots first.

"What's your name?" Brianna asked. And if the question was said too bluntly, the fact that she was asking while she was holding a pen and notebook in her hands, waiting to write down the answer, softened it not at all.

CHARM HIS PANTS OFF

"You know us, but we don't seem to know you," I said apologetically.

"Oh, I should've guessed," he said. "I'm Antoine Meunier. Sophie and I went to performing arts school together. We've known each other for years."

"You're also a dancer?" I asked. He had the lithe build of one. But I guessed not as the question made him blush.

"Only at the club on the weekends," he said. "I play piano."

"I think I've heard you play," I said.

"Really?" He sounded surprised.

"The music box that Sophie got for Christmas," I said. "The one that plays a digital recording. That was you."

"Yes it was," he said. "She played it for you?"

Not specifically. Brianna and I had been there when she had unwrapped it, and we had gotten a glimpse of it and heard the music play when she lifted the lid. But she had never explained a thing about it. But from the bright glow in Antoine's eyes, I saw how much it would mean to him, the idea that Sophie was showing off her gift proudly rather than hiding it away in her room.

"Yes," I said instead. "Come on; let's go back to the kitchen."

Sophie was setting dessert plates on the table as Brianna, and I led Antoine into the room. She glanced up at us, her eyes inscrutable, then promptly turned her attention back to the toaster oven that was gently reheating a half dozen pastries.

Antoine was still holding the rose, not sure what to do with it. I ducked into the butler's pantry and found the smallest of the crystal vases then filled it with water from the sink before handing it to him. I indicated which place was Sophie's at the table by a tilt of my head, and he gave me a smile and a nod of thanks.

Brianna fired up the electric kettle and counted out mugs and teabags. By the time the beignets were ready to come out of the toaster oven, the kettle was hissing then beeping its readiness.

"These look great," I said, all but snatching a plate from Sophie's hand the moment the pastry touched the china. "Sadly Brianna and I have a project we need to get back to. But if these taste as good as they smell, Auntie Claire's reputation is well-earned."

"I'll pass on your regards," Antoine said. Sophie glared at me as I snatched the next plate out of her hands and thrust it at Brianna. Her glower only deepened as I picked up my mug and followed Brianna back down the corridor.

"She didn't want to be alone with him," Brianna said to me.

"Tough," I said. "She's been dodging this too long. She doesn't even talk to us about it."

"Should she?" Brianna asked.

"We're her friends," I said, then, "hold up." Brianna stopped, one foot on the bottom step of the grand staircase, confusion on her face. "Let's sit in the parlor."

"Not the library?" she asked, as if the thought pained her.

"We won't be able to hear what's going on from the library," I said.

"I could always do a spell," Brianna said.

"That's too much like spying," I said, leading the way into the parlor and settling into one of the worn but comfortable chairs.

"And this isn't?" Brianna asked.

"This is just... potential eavesdropping," I said. I set my mug down then took my first bite of the warm beignet. I was promptly covered in a cloud of powdered sugar and pastry crumbs, all of which appeared to dodge the plate on my lap completely to dust my clothes.

So worth it, though. I could get new clothes. But I would never have another beignet like this one. My mind boggled at the idea of what it must have tasted like fresh.

"Why did you want us to leave Sophie alone if you want to know what they're saying?" Brianna asked. Then she took a bite of her own beignet, and even her formidable curiosity was stopped for just a moment in time as she closed her eyes in appreciation of the warmth and sweetness and richness filling her mouth.

"Don't you think it's odd she never mentioned Antoine to us before? He's clearly someone important to her," I said.

"From her old life," Brianna said. "You never talk about where you came from either."

14

"I send postcards to my foster grandparents," I said. "I've told you about them. You even know their names."

"Not their first names," Brianna said, pulling out her notebook to doublecheck.

"But you get my point," I said. "She never mentioned him to us at all. I know a lot more about your life back in Boston. I've even spoken with your mentor Sephora before."

"I'm an open book," Brianna agreed. "You not as much."

"I'd tell you anything you want to know, but frankly, no one in my hometown was remotely magical, so it's not really relevant. Not like you in Boston."

"Or Sophie in New Orleans?" Brianna said with a frown, then leaned closer to whisper, "do you think he knows she's a witch?"

"I don't think so," I said after taking a moment to replay every second I'd spent with him in my mind. "I think if he did, he'd know you and I are as well, and he would've acted differently. Had a different vibe or whatever."

"Maybe Sophie just wants to keep the magic and nonmagic parts of her life separate," Brianna said. "You've been struggling with that."

"And you haven't?" I asked.

Brianna shrugged. "I don't have any nonmagic parts of my life," she said.

I sighed. That was true. And I envied her. Being a witch and specifically having a calling to protect the magic portal that was the reason the school we were in existed had already crushed one budding possibly-more-than-a-friendship.

"So you think that's why she's so cold?" I asked.

"Cold?" she repeated, and I knew, absolutely knew, she was about to mention Sophie's new parka. But she caught herself in time. "She might want to keep a distance. I would think you of all people would understand that," she said. I nodded, but she didn't see me, attention focused on chasing the last of the crumbs around her plate, and she just had to complete her thought. "On account of Edward."

"This is different," I said. I'm not sure what made me more grumpy, the fact that Brianna had brought up Edward despite the unspoken agreement among the three of us not to mention that name or the fact that she had not even the lightest dusting of powdered sugar anywhere on her clothes. And she was wearing black pants and a dark green sweater. It would have shown. "Sophie and Antoine are in the same time."

"But different cities," Brianna said.

"It's not the same problem," I insisted.

Brianna just shrugged. "Perhaps to Sophie, it is."

There was a scraping of chairs from the direction of the kitchen and the happy rumble of Antoine's voice as he and Sophie came back down the corridor towards the foyer. I quickly grabbed a random book off the shelf beside my chair and pretended to be engrossed in the text while nursing the last of my tea.

Brianna didn't have to pretend to be engrossed, although it was still the plate on her lap that had all of her attention. That and, as usual, her own thoughts. Having felt a blast of those barely more than an hour earlier, I was amazed she was ever aware of the world around her at all.

"I wish I had a longer layover," Antoine was saying.

Sophie scoffed. "Explain to me again how there's any layover in Minneapolis, which is in no way between New Orleans and New York City?"

Antoine laughed. "Well. Auntie Claire was worried about you. I promised I'd check in."

"I write to Auntie Claire every Sunday," Sophie said, which was news to me.

"That's not the same as a phone call, you know," he said. "Or better, there's this new thing called a computer, and these computers will let you send an actual live video-"

"Haha," Sophie said.

"Seriously, though," Antoine said. "It would mean a lot for her to see you. You know if she could travel herself she'd've been here months ago."

"I know," Sophie said. "I'll try."

I waited for Antoine to quote Yoda to her, but he didn't. He just nodded as if that was an acceptable answer then turned his attention to pulling on his still wet boots.

"Your clothes are all wrong for this climate," Sophie said. She was speaking not exactly warmly, but nowhere near as chilly as she'd been when he'd first arrived.

And yet, when he straightened and tried to step closer to her, arms opening to embrace her, she took a step back. He dropped his arms.

For a moment, I thought he was going to call her out, but instead, he summoned that bright smile and directed it at her again. "Lucky for me, I don't live in this climate."

"Manhattan can't be much warmer," Sophie said. Then, almost as if she couldn't help herself, she started fussing with the draping of his scarf around his neck and shoulders, tucking it closer around his exposed ears. "People in New York also wear hats."

"Some do," he said.

"You're being vain about your hair," she said with a frown.

"I'm not!" he said with a laugh. "Well, maybe a little. But I tell you what; you send me a hat. Any hat at all. If it's from you, I swear I'll never take it off."

Sophie gave a short laugh at that, then started shooing him out the door. He caught her arm but seemed to change his mind and let her go.

I had the nearly overwhelming urge to call him back, to make him stay. I knew it would only need another hour or two for him to melt Sophie's heart completely. I could see it in the way she was leaning towards the door, as if a part of her longed to follow him.

He had barely stepped off the front mat when he spun back around. For a moment, I thought I had done magic without knowing it, put some sort of compulsion spell on him. But it was nothing to do with me.

"Your mother!" he said, stepping back to catch both of Sophie's hands. "How could I have forgotten to ask?"

"My mother?" Sophie echoed, as if sounding out syllables that had no meaning for her.

"Your mother. That was the whole reason you came here. You said

17

they might know something here, that they might be able to help you find out what happened to her. I can't believe I totally forgot to ask if you made any progress on that. I didn't mean to hit you full blast with nothing but my life and all. That was totally insensitive of me. But I really do have to run. Just tell me, Sophie. Any news?"

"No news," Sophie said. She still sounded like she'd just taken a severe blow to the head and words were foreign to her.

"I'm so sorry," he said, and this time when he pulled her towards him, she let him put his arms around her and squeeze her tight. "Promise me you'll call and we can talk about it. I never meant to act like I was ignoring all that. You gave up everything to come here, and I just let it slide by me."

"It's all right," Sophie said, and her arms tightened around him. "I wanted to hear about you. It was good to hear your voice again."

"Then call me," he said earnestly.

"I will. I'll try," Sophie said.

I focused on the book on my lap, desperate to give them a moment's privacy without creating the distraction of trying to leave the room. Alas, the book was in French. And upside-down.

Then I heard the door close again. This time the click of the latch had an air of finality to it. As if the world was a different place now than it was before Antoine came to call.

And from the look on Sophie's face as she stepped into the parlor, it really was.

CHAPTER 3

*B*rianna and I both leaped to our feet and guided Sophie to one of the chairs, as she looked in danger of just crumpling to the floor. Brianna pushed the last of her tea into Sophie's hands. Sophie took the mug but didn't attempt to drink from it.

"I'm sorry," I said. "I suppose seeing him brought back a lot of homesickness."

"And you miss him," Brianna added.

Sophie was looking down into the cold remains of the tea in the mug in her hands, but she looked up at the two of us as if we had both gone crazy.

"You're not upset about Antoine?" I guessed.

"No," she said, then took a breath. Her eyes came into sharper focus. "Well, yes, but that's not it. Didn't you hear what he said?"

"About your mother?" I said.

"Yes," Sophie said forcefully.

"But why would you be upset about your mother?" Brianna asked. "From what Antoine said, it sounded like she's been gone a long time. Not that that isn't upsetting, but you seem closer to something like shock. An acute condition, not chronic."

"Oh, this is acute," Sophie said. She took a drink of tea, grimaced, then set the mug aside. "You don't understand. He said those words out loud, 'your mother,' and all of a sudden I realized, I can't remember the last time I even thought of my mother. Isn't that strange?"

"Is it?" I asked. I couldn't remember the last time I had thought about my mother, either. It didn't come up much. I looked at Brianna, who frowned and shrugged.

"It is," Sophie insisted. "Because I know Antoine is right. I came here for specific reasons, but one of the big ones was to find out what happened to my mother. And yet somehow, I just... forgot."

"We have been pretty busy," Brianna said. "We have more than a job; we have a calling. Even when we're not physically focused on working magic or practicing magic or researching magic, we're still focused on that calling. It doesn't leave a lot of time for other thoughts."

"But this isn't just forgetting to think about her," Sophie said. "Antoine mentioned her, and I remembered that I forgot, but..." She broke off, pressing the back of her hand to her lips as if holding back a sob. "I can't remember her even now. Only a few images, nothing important. And I can't feel anything about her at all." She took a deep breath, holding back another sob.

"Sophie," I said, putting a hand on her shoulder and giving it a squeeze. "Maybe it's just stress. You've been working so hard."

"It's not just Sophie," Brianna said. We both looked up at her, standing over us with her arms crossed. "I just tried remembering my own mother. I can remember a few facts like her name and when she died. I can get a couple of images, but they're blurry. I can't remember her face at all."

"And the emotions?" Sophie asked, wiping at her eyes.

"None," Brianna said. "Nothing feels missing. It's like this was all the memory I ever had. And yet, how can that be true? I wish I had a control to compare it to. Like a journal or something."

"Amanda?" Sophie said to me.

I sat back down in my chair and closed my eyes. "I never knew her name," I said. I was certain that was true. "She never spoke, I remember that too. My wand comes from the tree where my father died and where she birthed me, almost at the same moment."

"But do you remember her?" Sophie asked.

I pressed my hands over my closed eyes, as if more darkness would help. But finally I had to give up, dropping my hands and shaking my head. "No. I think she had long blonde hair? But I'm not sure. She only died a few years ago, not back when I was a kid. I should have more memories than this."

"What's going on?" Sophie asked. "Is this part of the calling? Now that we have to serve our purpose here, the rest of our lives just disappear?"

"No," Brianna said. "You remembered Antoine."

"Maybe we only forget the dead?" I suggested.

"But I don't know that my mother is actually dead," Sophie said. "She might be alive. That was the biggest reason why I came here when Cynthia Thomas invited me to come. I was hoping to find out what had happened to her."

"Maybe it has something to do with the school itself," Brianna said. Suddenly she was looking as distressed as Sophie and I were. "I can't remember. I can't make myself remember. But didn't our mothers all go here?"

"The same class," Sophie said.

"The last class," I added.

"Does that mean something?" Brianna wondered.

"Maybe Mr. Trevor would know?" I said.

"He doesn't really understand magic," Brianna said.

"Not magic," Sophie said, "but surely he knows something about our mothers."

"It can't hurt to ask," I said.

I don't think any of us had ever knocked on the door to Mr. Trevor's personal office before. I had only ever gotten a brief glimpse of its interior, that first day when he gave me a tour of the house. He certainly looked surprised to see us all standing there, especially as Sophie's eyes were red from crying.

"Is something the matter?" he asked.

21

"We wanted to ask you about our mothers," I said.

"Your mothers?"

"Yes," I said. "We were hoping you remembered them."

"But I told you all when you came," he said, looking at each of us in turn. "I started helping my father out here in the school several years after your mothers left the school."

"Left," Brianna said, "not graduate?"

"Well," Mr. Trevor said, chewing at his lip. "There is no graduation per se."

"So you don't remember them at all?" I asked.

"Well, as I said, I never knew them," he said. "But I remember things about them."

"Like what?" Brianna asked.

"Oh, Miss Zenobia would tell me stories of her former students from time to time," he said with a soft smile. "Some clever thing one girl said. An ingenious invention by another. That sort of thing."

"You don't remember anything specific?" Sophie asked.

"I don't know I ever knew much to begin with," he said. "Miss Zenobia was fond of them, that I know. That's why you three were called on to take her place. She was very clear about that. No other students had the potential your mothers had."

"Then why did she ever let them leave?" Sophie asked.

"That I don't know," he admitted. "But she kept their class photo in the place of honor outside her office. I often caught her looking at it. There was always something wistful in her face when I would find her standing there in front of that photo. Well, you can see it yourself, just down there."

We looked at each other then walked back down the hall to where a photo in a simple wooden frame hung on the wall opposite the locked door to Miss Zenobia's office. I glanced at Brianna then at Sophie. I could tell they were thinking the same thing I was.

How many times had we walked past this portrait and never once glanced at it, let alone given it a proper examination?

And now we were standing in front of it. There were only twelve girls gathered on the front porch for the portrait. And yet I had no idea which of the three with long, blonde hair was my mother. Perhaps none of them. Perhaps I was wrong even about the hair.

"Girls?" Mr. Trevor asked, concerned. Sophie was crying again, and even Brianna looked like her confusion was about to spill over into tears.

"Can you tell us who is who?" I asked.

"The names are written on the plaque over here," he said, pointing to a slate propped up on a stand on the left of the picture. "Here is your mother, Amanda. Kathleen Stinson. And yours, Brianna. Lula Collins. And right in front is Marie DuBois."

Sophie raised her hand, brushing the image of her mother's face with a stroke of her fingertip.

"I don't know what you two are feeling," Brianna said, "but I feel very strange. I look at her face, and it matches up with the name in my head, but the connection is so... clinical. Like I'm remembering what actor played a part in a movie I had never even liked. And I still don't remember anything else about her."

"My name isn't even Clarke?" I said, then gave myself a shake. That wasn't relevant. "I think I'm in the same boat as Brianna. The analytical part of my brain is making the connection, but there's no emotional subtext to it at all."

"Sophie?" Brianna asked.

"That's her," Sophie said, "and yet, I still don't remember her. Even as I'm looking right at her." Then she gasped and retracted her hand as if the glass of the picture frame had scalded her.

"What is it?" I asked, but she just pointed at the slate.

I scanned the names, certain she must have reacted that way because another of the names was familiar. Evanora, perhaps. But they were all perfectly ordinary, perfectly anonymous.

I was about to scan it a third time when I finally saw, and I too gasped out loud.

"What is it?" Brianna asked, tortured to be left out.

I turned to Mr. Trevor as I planted my fingertip on the photo. "Class of 1966? There was no way my mother was that old."

"What's going on?" Sophie moaned, clutching at her head. She was putting her hair in total disarray, and for the first time since I'd met her, it was staying that way, a chaotic swirl atop her head.

"What *is* going on?" Mr. Trevor asked.

"Something not right," I said. "We've all just realized we've not once thought of our mothers since we came here, and now that we're trying to think of them, or memories are gone. Like they were wiped, but imperfectly. Fragments remain."

"But no feelings," Sophie said.

"But what could do such a thing?" Mr. Trevor asked, shocked.

"Magic," Brianna said, a determined look to her face.

"Does this happen to students here?" I asked.

"No, never," Mr. Trevor said. "Why would it?"

"Why, indeed?" Brianna pondered.

"That's not the important question," I said.

"What is the important question?" Sophie asked.

"The important question is who," I said.

CHAPTER 4

*B*rianna was bustling around the library, moving around the large center table that was her usual workstation and consulting this or that page from an open tome then diving deeper into the stacks to find some other more obscure text.

Sophie and I knew from long experience that even if we understood the way the books were ordered in the library and were capable of helping out, Brianna would find the need to articulate what she was looking for to be maddeningly distracting to her mental processes.

There was nothing we could do but wait while Brianna whatever it was she was looking for. Which was hard for me, but for Sophie looked to be pure torture. She kept grabbing at her hair, which was already standing on end. I hadn't seen her do a single thing to her clothes, but somehow her entire appearance had downgraded from her usual perfectly crisp and brightly clean look to something... well, I wouldn't say slovenly, but only because it reminded me of what I saw in the mirror most days.

"This is insane," Sophie said, looking at me with wild eyes. I caught her hands to keep her from having another go at her hair.

"It's strange, but we'll figure it out," I said. "I'm glad Antoine came.

Who knows how long we would've gone on, not remembering our own mothers, if he hadn't said what he did?"

"I didn't want him to come," Sophie said, turning away from me to start furiously pacing the small space between the last row of bookshelves and the doors out to the front porch. "I asked him not to. I need to keep him away from all of this."

"Why?" I asked.

Sophie stopped dead in her tracks and stood frozen for the third time that day. I was just reaching out to touch her shoulder when she spun to look at me. "I don't know. I thought I did, right up until you asked me. My mouth opened to answer, but the words weren't there. I don't know why, but I'm still absolutely certain it's important. What's happening to me?"

"Does it feel like what I get sometimes?" I asked. "That compulsion that kept me in Scandia until Cynthia Thomas came?"

"Maybe," Sophie said. "I don't know how that feels for you." She hugged her arms around herself tightly. "I've been telling him not to come here since I got here. I've had this feeling at least that long. Which seems to also be about the time I forgot that I was looking for my mother. Is it related?"

"Maybe," I said. "Hopefully when Brianna pulls this spell together, we'll get a better picture of things."

"I hope so," Sophie said. "But I doubt it's going to explain everything. If something is making us forget our mothers, and making me keep Antoine away, I can see how that could be connected. But what about the other thing? The fact that our mothers were students here in the 60s? That's got to be something else entirely."

"Well, time travel isn't so strange for us," I said.

"But we only go back to one time, and it isn't the 60s," Sophie said. She started pacing again, but more slowly, and still hugging herself as if the room had gone cold. She looked like a lost child, the sweater that had fit her perfectly that morning now hanging from her like a stretched out, shapeless garment.

I didn't know how to make her feel better. Maybe it would just take time.

"You can still call Antoine," I said. "He might not even be as far as the airport yet. I'm sure he'd come right back if you asked him to."

"Why would I do that?" Sophie asked.

"If you've been driving him away for no reason, I just thought maybe you'd want to talk to him again and explain. Or just have him there for comfort or something?"

Sophie pondered. Then she straightened her shoulders and smoothed her hands over her hair. "No. I'm OK."

"Are you sure?"

"Yes," she said, and she was sounding more like her usual self. "I don't know the reason I wanted him away from me, but I still think there might be one. Maybe when Brianna helps us figure this all out, I'll remember what it is. In the meantime, seeing him again is just going to be more awkward. I can't explain things to him at all."

"He doesn't know you're a witch?" I asked.

"No. That much I do remember about my mother: she always insisted on complete secrecy," she said.

"I think I'm ready," Brianna said, coming towards us with a glass sphere carefully balanced on top of a pile of heavy books. Sophie grabbed the sphere before it could roll off its perch.

"Should we take this outside?" I asked.

"No need," Brianna said. "It's not related to the time portal, so we can work here."

"Where it's warm," Sophie said.

"Yes," Brianna agreed. "Amanda, there's a chain of yarn in my pocket..." She hiked the books in her arms a little higher until I found the bundle of yarn in her sweater pocket and pulled it out. Although it was an even shade of red and crocheted from a smooth, well-spun yarn, I knew it had been carded and died and spun and crocheted all by Brianna's own hands down in the cellar.

"What's this for?" I asked.

"Use it to make a circle on the floor here," Brianna said. "We'll all sit inside it to contain the magic. Just in case whatever I find turns out to be malevolent."

"And this?" Sophie asked, rolling the sphere from palm to palm.

27

"In case whatever we're poking at needs to be contained," Brianna said. She waited for me to line up the yarn chain behind her in a gentle arc before settling down in a cross-legged posture and arranging the books around her.

When I reached the end of the yarn I had made a circle just large enough to contain the three of us sitting with knees touching, Brianna's books tucked mostly under her own legs, the sphere in the center of the three of us.

"First we need to cast the circle," Brianna said. "We need to make it a separate space from the rest of the world around us. It shouldn't be too hard; it's just a tiny variation of what we do in meditation."

"Just make it a circle around the three of us," Sophie said, but she didn't look like she quite grasped it.

"More like a sphere, really," Brianna said. "The yarn circle is just a visual cue of where that sphere intersects the floor. I'll say some words, but you should think of your protective winds defining that boundary. And Amanda, weave it with threads."

"All right," I agreed and closed my eyes.

This time, when Sophie's warm breeze blew over me, I knew the baked goods I was smelling were Auntie Claire's beignets. And I could feel the pang of homesickness that squeezed her heart, but she put it aside to focus on the spell. When I turned my attention to the world of threads, I found them already moving around as if to protect us. I only made a few tweaks to the arrangement before going back to my body and its more mundane awareness.

"All right," Brianna said, looking down at the page of the book tucked under her left knee. "Take my hands and flow your power into me. I'll say the words of the spell, and then we'll see what happens."

I put my hand left hand in hers, then took Sophie's hand in my right. This part was very familiar. We'd been practicing it a lot. I had learned to hold back the full force of what longed to flow out of me. It had been a long time since I'd burned either of them, and even though we had never attempted to use that power for anything as big as what we were doing now, I was determined that I wasn't going to slip up.

Brianna chanted words over and over, words so strange my mind refused to even make out the sounds of their syllables. It was a good thing she didn't want us to repeat them after her because even though I could hear the repetition and knew it was only maybe a dozen sounds, they wouldn't stick in my mind at all.

I looked up at Sophie, hoping to get a sense if she felt the same confusion, and was startled by the impression that I was looking at some sort of overlapping image. I could, with great focus, see the world of threads and the mundane world at once, layered on top of each other, but it was a strain. This wasn't that, but I was definitely seeing something like a thick, dark cloud overlapping the top of her head. It was both there and wasn't.

Sophie felt my gaze on her and looked up. Her eyes widened, her focus more on my forehead than my own eyes, and I was certain she saw something going on with the top of my head too.

We both looked to Brianna, who had stopped chanting. Brianna looked from me to Sophie then back again, more with intellectual interest than with shock.

"What is it?" Sophie asked. Her hand twitched in mine, as if she wanted to reach up and touch whatever it was.

"The spell made manifest," Brianna said.

"So someone did cast a spell on us," Sophie said.

"Yes, this was deliberate," Brianna said. "It has intentionality. We didn't just accidentally trip one of Miss Zenobia's old wards somewhere in the house or anything."

"But why don't we remember the spell happening?" I asked.

"Because it's still there, in our brains," Sophie said. "It's no wonder I can't think straight. Look at it."

"Can't we get rid of it?" I asked.

"It gets tricky," Brianna said. She wrinkled up her nose and crossed her eyes, and the cloud in her brain jostled then settled back down. "We can't dispel our own brain fogs, but two of us working together can pull it out of the mind of the third."

"Let's do Brianna first," Sophie said, and I nodded my agreement. Brianna being clear-headed was definitely a priority."

"Focus on drawing it out but putting it into the glass sphere," Brianna said. "Don't let it slip away from you."

"Got it," I said, closing my eyes. In the world of threads, I could see the darkly glowing filaments resting in the shining web of her mind, like the scribble of an angry child. They were tangled among her own threads, but I gently separated them out, aided by a warm breeze that I couldn't feel, no longer actually being in my body, but I could see as it softly blew through the threads.

Then Brianna was free. I opened my eyes.

"Oh," Brianna said, blinking.

"Tell us," Sophie said.

"No, not yet," Brianna said. "Let's get Amanda free first, and then you, and then we'll talk."

They both turned their attention to me. I fought the urge to tense up, as if I were about to come under a surgical knife. Sophie's magic was easy to relax into. Brianna's magic was more like little brass instruments working in my brain, but I could feel how deft she was in her work.

It felt like losing a scab that had dried so tightly it was pulling all the skin around it. Now my mind was coming free, little by little. Then it was gone entirely. I saw the cloud floating past my nose to sink to the floor, joining Brianna's little cloud already in the sphere.

And I remembered. All at once, a flood of images from as profound as the day my mother had died in my arms to as mundane as baking cookies on a rainy afternoon while listening to Buddy Holly on the radio.

"I remember," I said, my vision starting to swim.

"Sophie now," Brianna said. I nodded, but the tears wouldn't stop coming. "Amanda."

I took a deep breath and, as much as it killed me to do it, pushed the memories aside. "I'm ready," I said.

I focused on the scribble of threads in Sophie's brain, this time aided not by a dancing breeze but as if by surgical instruments I couldn't see except by their effects. Brianna let me take the lead, somehow sensing when I was going to turn my attention to this fila-ment or that knot, and she would lift it or scrape something away.

Then it was done, sealed inside the glass sphere with the other two. I opened my eyes, suddenly acutely exhausted. Magic was so tiring.

"Sophie?" Brianna called softly.

Sophie still had her eyes closed, but tears were spilling out between her lashes. Then she tugged on our hands, and we all went from sitting with our hands joined to kneeling in the center of the circle in a tight hug. And even Brianna was crying now.

CHAPTER 5

I don't know how long we stayed like that, just holding each other. We weren't trading magic at the moment, and yet I could still feel the tangle of emotions running through all of us. Happiness, at having our memories back. Sadness from the memories themselves. But soon those collapsed down into just two things: confusion over what exactly had happened to us, and resolve to figure it out.

We sat back, no longer even holding hands but still within the magic circle we had conjured. The three clouds were now one, swirling darkly within the confines of the glass sphere. Brianna pulled one of the books onto her lap and started turning pages.

"I never knew my mother's name," I said. "Not until today, when Mr. Trevor showed us that photograph. Whoever put this spell on us, it must have been that very first day. I still don't understand how I just forgot to ask even that much when I got here."

"I don't remember the moment of the spell hitting us either," Brianna said, her eyes on the book as she scanned page after page.

"My father died in a car crash the day I was born," I said. "No one knew who they were or where they were going. But I kind of think now, driving that fast in that weather, they must have been running away from something. But what?"

"My mother was always looking over her shoulder," Sophie said. "She taught me that. Always keep my senses open, always stay hidden. If either of us felt anything even remotely magical, we'd run. I was better at sensing magic than she was. Even when I was just a toddler, long before I started kindergarten, she trusted me implicitly. If I felt something, we'd run."

"Maybe they were both being pursued by the same person, or group of people?" I suggested. We looked to Brianna, who was still focused on the book but sensed the lull in the conversation around her.

"Nothing like that with us," she said. "But we lived in an insular community."

"Surrounded by witches?" I asked.

Brianna looked up as she considered. "A few powerful witches like Sephora, although I didn't meet Sephora until I was in college. But my mother's coven had three witches of that level. The others were more witch-friendly. They had no real magic, but they were sensitive to it. Knowing what I know now, I think they might have been protecting us. We didn't go out into the world much."

"But no one ever went after my mother after the accident," I said. "We just lived normal lives. No magic."

"My mother died when I was six. The witches that looked after me kept me at home until I was old enough for junior high, but after that, I was out in the world all day, then back in their world at night. I don't remember ever feeling any danger or like I was being watched or followed," Brianna said.

"I always felt watched," Sophie said. "But I never saw anyone. I just felt the magic and ran. Maybe I was just being paranoid. But my mother did disappear. She just went out one evening to get something from the corner store and never came back."

"Did you sense anything? I guess I don't know how big your range is," I said.

"I could open myself up and feel magic for blocks and blocks,"

Sophie said. "I think I can do more now, especially when we're working together. But even then, I could sense magic much further away than the corner store. But I felt nothing. And no one saw anything. The police investigation went nowhere. I would've been in foster care if not for Auntie Claire. Who technically isn't even my aunt."

"What about your dads?" I asked. "Mine died in that car crash, and I guess I still don't know his first name. But what about you?"

They both shook their heads.

"My mother didn't like to talk about it," Sophie said. "She said it wasn't safe."

"My mom would just get sad," Brianna said. "But she wouldn't tell me anything. So I don't know his name either."

"Nor I," Sophie said.

"And do we know how old our mothers were?" I asked. They shook their heads. "No drivers licenses or nothing? In my case, my mother's identity was never confirmed. She didn't speak, and she had amnesia after the crash. If she had any memory of before it, she never gave a clue. My foster grandparents, the Schneidermans, named her Willow for the tree the car hit, but the date of birth on her government paperwork was just an estimate."

"I never saw any paperwork," Sophie said. "No drivers license either."

"Me neither," Brianna said.

"That picture in the hallway looks like what my mom looked like when I was born, or pretty close," I said.

"Same," Brianna said, her eyes back on the book.

"I don't have pictures," Sophie said. "My earliest memories... her hair was different, but I would guess she was only a few years older. Certainly not three decades older."

"And our own birthdays?" I asked. "Mine is August 10, 1997."

"March 2, 1998," Brianna said.

"January 16, 1999," Sophie said.

"You didn't tell us it was your birthday!" Brianna said.

"Really? That's what we're going to focus on?" Sophie asked.

"You keep a lot of secrets, Sophie," I said. "Was that another compulsion? Not to tell us we had a lovely excuse for a cake and ice cream and decorations?"

"I don't like a fuss," Sophie said.

"A fuss can be a nice distraction from all of this darkness," I said and looked down at the roiling cloud inside the glass sphere. What were we going to do with that?

"Your birthday might be the most significant one," Brianna said to me.

"Why's that?" I asked. It was still months and months away.

"Well, you're the oldest of the three of us for one," Brianna said. "Plus, if your mother really was actively fleeing something, that might be a clue. If the three of them had done something together, it might have happened just before that."

"What would they have done? Who were they running from?" I asked.

"Was it in 1966 or 1997?" Sophie added.

"All good questions," Brianna said, but she had that distracted quality to her voice, like something in the book was hogging most of her attention.

"Are we sure we have all of our memories back?" I asked. "There are still so many things we don't know."

"It doesn't feel like anything is missing," Sophie said. "I remember my mom. She was secretive. And yours never talked. We can't remember things we never knew."

"You don't know if your mother is alive or dead, right?" I said. "Maybe we can look for her. If we could find her, we could ask her all these questions."

"I'd love to do that," Sophie said. "But she disappeared in New Orleans. And we can't leave here."

"Not now," Brianna said. "But maybe someday."

"I hate feeling trapped," I grumbled. "I feel useless."

"We have things we can do," Brianna said, finally closing the book with a clap. "Someone put this spell on us for a reason. Someone wanted us to forget our mothers for a reason. We might remember more as things come back to us. Pay attention to your dreams for sure; there might be scraps there."

"Surely that's not all we can do," I said, itching for a foe to fight.

"Not at all," Brianna said. "The why might take a while to figure out, but in the meantime, we can figure out the how, and that might lead us to the who."

"You want to figure out how these clouds got into our brains in the first place?" Sophie asked.

"And figuring that out will probably tell us who did it," Brianna said.

"And when," I added, thinking of Evanora, biding her time in 1928.

"So how do we figure out the how?" Sophie asked.

A slow grin spread across Brianna's face as she pulled out her wand.

"We start by dropping our magic circle and smashing that glass," she said, pointing at the cloud-filled bauble.

CHAPTER 6

"*W*ait!" I cried even as power was beginning to crackle all around Brianna's wand. She dissipated it with a flick of her wrist.

"What?" she asked.

"Remember what happened with the locator spell that led us to the hatpin?" I asked. "That thing moved so fast. I want to be down by the time portal before you break the glass, in case it goes back over the bridge to the past."

"I don't see how the spell could've worked that way," Brianna said with a frown. "Memory spells are very tricky, and strictly short range attacks."

"But we never saw an attacker," Sophie said.

"No, but there must have been a trigger," Brianna said. "And assuming the simplest solution, it must have been something that hit all three of us at once."

"A trigger, like a bomb?" I asked.

"Maybe more like a tripwire," Sophie said.

"More like that," Brianna agreed.

"So the three of us together set off a magical tripwire?" I asked. "But when?"

"I don't remember anything like that," Sophie said.

"It may have been something super subtle," Brianna said. "An enchanted sugar bowl when we were all drinking tea together."

"Or anytime we ate dinner," Sophie said.

"Was it something we ate?" I asked. "A magical parasite hatched inside of us and made that?" I pointed at the swirling mass inside the glass sphere.

"It's a possibility," Brianna said. "But I think tripwire might be closer. Someone not here had to have a way to be sure of the timing."

"And when you say someone, we're all thinking of Evanora, right?" I said.

"Or her mysterious employer," Sophie said.

"We know she has access to the present," I said. "Or she did have in November, and probably still does now. But did she earlier than that?"

"If she can do it at all, I don't know why it would have started only in November," Brianna said.

"Amanda drew her attention to the present," Sophie said.

"I never said a word that would lead her to that conclusion," I said.

"We're not going to find the answers to this through discussion and argument," Brianna said. "We have to smash the sphere."

"No, I have to smash the sphere," Sophie said.

"Is this a revenge thing?" Brianna asked.

"No," Sophie said. "It has to be me because Amanda is going to be watching the threads that form the time portal, and you're going to be back there making sure the wards we put on that wardrobe are as strong as ever."

"The wardrobe," I said, having pretty much forgotten it existed. "Can a witch cast spells through it?"

"I don't know," Brianna admitted. "That's why I put so many wards on it."

"Maybe we should have destroyed it rather than keep it," I said.

"No," Sophie said. "We still might need it. Today or someday."

"In the meantime," Brianna said, getting up from the floor, "I'll check all the wards first, then when I yell you can smash the sphere and we'll see what happens."

"I'll get down to the time portal," I said. Sophie drew her wand and aimed it at the sphere as if warning it to behave.

Brianna was halfway across the library when a thought struck her, and she turned to look back. "Amanda, you're not going to be able to hear the signal to go."

"I'll be watching," I said. "I'll see."

"Don't cross the bridge without us," she said. "Even if it rushes past you. Don't go back to the past alone."

"I won't," I promised, hoping that my resolve on that wouldn't be put to the test.

I quickly exchanged house slippers for boots and pulled on my coat, still getting my hat and gloves on as I tramped across the snow to the orchard. We had a nice little path formed from our daily treks, although if we got any more snow, I'd have to stop calling it a path because it was already closer to a trench.

Once under the fruit trees, I pulled the hood up over my hat to block out the wind. This confined my vision to a narrow tunnel directly in front of me, but that didn't matter. A single breath and a closing of my eyes was all it took for me to get to the world of threads these days.

I looked to the bridge first. I had examined it just that morning and had noticed nothing unusual about it then, but I was looking with a different eye this time. Was there anything in there like the scribble that had been within our brains? Anything I noticed now with my memory restored that I hadn't noticed this morning still under the effects of the brain cloud?

I still didn't see anything off, but I felt uneasy. That cloud had been in my brain for longer than I had known I was a witch. Every time I had tried a spell or even just opened myself up to the magic in the world around me, that spell had been in there, fogging my brain. How could that not make everything I thought I knew suspect?

I turned my attention to the charm school, always a bright glow of magical threads. Small objects of power filled the rooms, especially Miss Zenobia Weekes' office, but it was more than that. The walls themselves had a power. I knew this from the very first time I had touched magic. The only reason I was still alive now was that power flowing from the house itself into me. It had saved me. And then that power had returned to the house. It was there now.

We might need to find a way to call on that more deliberately. I made a mental note to talk to Brianna about it later.

At the moment I could easily pick out the places where threads coalesced into the people I knew best in the world. Mr. Trevor, closest to me in his office. Brianna, near the complex twisting of threads and knots that formed her wards, so dense I could sense nothing of the wardrobe I knew was within. Then Sophie herself, and beside Sophie, the angry scribble that even as I looked was released from its confinement.

I don't hear things in the world of threads, but something was buzzing in my head like a nest of angry wasps. The scribble couldn't make a sound that would travel to me, but somehow it was conveying its anger to me.

The bright threads that formed Sophie moved back from the scribble as it expanded, but as it expanded it became less and less dense. It flowed around Sophie, not a single scribbled filament inter-acting with her threads. It was giving her and her power a wide berth.

Then it reached the walls of the library itself, and then the expansion sped up. In the blink of an eye it was distributed through the house, hiding within the walls, the angry scribbles pulled thin to the finest of lines that were almost, but not quite, impossible to discern.

I stood out in the yard, looking at the house for quite some time. It was clear the spell wasn't going to try to get past me to the time portal. It wasn't moving at all. But still, I stood there, examining every bit of the house over and over again.

Did it look different than when I had looked at it before? Or was it the same?

I felt like it was the same, but I couldn't be entirely sure. I had never looked so closely at the walls of the house before, at the power that pulsed quietly through every brick and bit of plaster. The lines of the spell were so thin, so easy to overlook, especially now that they lay so quietly dormant.

I turned my attention back to the bridge. I had seen something similar before when I had watched Juno disappear into the fabric of the time portal. Was this something she had done?

No, I didn't think so. She had asked me to be her student, her protégée. And she had asked me that months after I'd come to the school. She might have the power to cast a spell to tamper with our memories, but I felt like she would have saved that until after she'd tried to win me over after I had turned her down.

Finally, I went back into the house, hung up my coat, and set my boots near the radiator to dry. Mr. Trevor was in the kitchen just turning on the oven.

Right. It was still Valentine's Day.

"Is everything all right, Miss Amanda?" he asked.

"Yeah," I said. "We got our memories back."

"Excellent," he said. "Do you know how they were lost?"

"Not lost, taken," I said, with perhaps more vitriol than I intended. "We're working on who did it."

"Another mystery to be solved," he said.

"Yeah. Not a murder this time, though."

"A theft."

"Maybe more like a heist? It seems pretty elaborate. We'll tell you all about it once we figure it out ourselves."

"I have complete confidence in the three of you. Everyone still planning for dinner?"

"Definitely," I said. "We might have a few things to finish up first, though. Might have to step out for a bit."

"Here," Mr. Trevor said, disappearing behind the refrigerator door then emerging with a plate of cheese and cold cuts covered in plastic wrap. "If you've been doing magic, you're going to want some protein and fat."

"Perfect," I said, taking the plate. "Thanks."

I probably should have waited until I got upstairs, but I hadn't realized how ravenous I was until I had that plate in my hands. I did manage to confine my nibbling to a few squares of cheese that were near the edge of the plate, clearly in danger of being dropped on the steps.

Working magic did make me super hungry, but you could always count on Mr. Trevor to have planned ahead.

"Anything?" Brianna asked the moment I was in the doorway.

"What did you see?" I asked, setting the plate on the newspaper table and peeling back the rest of the wrap. We all rolled cheese and cold cuts together and started eating before we spoke again.

"Nothing with the wardrobe," Brianna said. "I felt like something moved around me. Like literally pulled apart to move around me without touching me."

"Pretty much what I saw," I said.

"It's still here, right?" Sophie said, looking all around. "In the walls."

"In the walls," I agreed.

"But was it always here?" she asked, then looked directly at me to be sure I knew the question wasn't merely rhetorical.

"That I don't know," I admitted. "But I have a plan."

"I don't think I'm going to like this plan," Brianna said with a frown.

"We just need to make a short trip back to 1928," I said. "Quick as a flash. I just need a look. And I didn't do it without you two-"

"You don't get cookies for doing what we agreed," Brianna said sharply. Sophie looked at the plate as if cookies might be hidden there.

"One quick look. Then we come back up here and process all the data we have," I said.

"We can't let this go," Sophie said, because Brianna was still looking like she wanted to argue against it. "Someone tried to take our memories from us. And if they could do that, we could be sitting ducks here for whatever else they want to roll out next. We have to know so we can protect ourselves."

"All right," Brianna said. "But we stick together, we're only there for a moment, and we're warded against witches."

"Warded against witches?" I asked. "How long is that going to take."

"No time at all," Brianna said. "Up until now it was just a little side project, but I've been working on a thing since New Year's."

"What thing?" Sophie asked.

"Well, remember Cynthia's amulet?" Brianna asked. "The one that did so much more than just let her cross the time bridge?"

I looked up at Sophie. I was pretty sure the grin on my own face was a match to the one she was sporting.

The theft of our memories might have been of heist-like scope and complexity, but it was starting to feel like we could summon up a nice counter-heist of our own.

This might end up being kind of fun.

CHAPTER 7

*B*rianna had attempted this sort of protective magic before. She had made me a cloaking spell in the form of an actual cloak that had kept me safe enough for a short trip back to 1928 to talk to Coco, but she hadn't had enough confidence in it to let me use it again.

I had considered taking that cloak on more than one occasion, using it plus Cynthia's amulet to hide me long enough to slip back in time. Not to meet Edward, because that would be too hard, but just to see him from a distance. To be sure he was all right. The desire had kept me up nights.

And that whole time Brianna had been tinkering away on a secret project without a word to anyone. Or at least, without a word to me.

"Did you know about this?" I asked as Sophie, and I followed Brianna down the steps to the cellar.

"I saw her working on something, but she's always working on something," Sophie said. "When's the last time you were down here?"

"I'm down here all the time," I said. "Doing and redoing all the steps to rebond with my wand."

"More like staying away from the cellar to avoid your wand," Sophie said.

"If it were your wand, you'd know what it feels like when it betrays you," I said.

"Have you considered that your attitude might be why it won't rebond with you?" Sophie asked. "I'm not trying to be mean. It's an honest question."

I bit back the retort that wanted to explode out of me and forced myself to really think about the answer.

"I've been open to it," I said. "It feels like if anything, it's too eager to bond with me again. It really feels like it answers to someone else now."

"Maybe leave it home this trip, then," Sophie said.

"I'm still researching that," Brianna said to us as we gathered around her workbench.

"My wand?" I asked.

"Yes. The fact that it's not responding correctly to any of the usual methods makes me suspicious too," she said. "There's more wrong than just another witch briefly handling it. But I don't know what else could have happened."

"Hence the research," I said. "I can help with that. I should help with that."

"The books are pretty... esoteric," Brianna said. "But in the meantime..." She took a bundle wrapped in dark cloth out of a drawer and set it on the bench, then carefully spread out the corners of the velvet.

There were two fine gold chains resting on the cloth. One chain was attached to a disc of creamy jade, the other a golden pocket watch, the kind where you could see all of the gears at work inside of it.

"The jade and the watch were both in Miss Zenobia's jewelry box," Brianna said, speaking softly, almost reverently.

"She had a jewelry box?" Sophie asked.

"I'm guessing these objects are part of why Mr. Trevor told me not to touch anything my first day here," I said.

"They had some latent magic within them, yes," Brianna agreed. "I spent a long time searching for just the right pieces that would take up the spells most readily."

"There are only two," Sophie said.

"We only need two," I said, pulling down on my collar so she could see Cynthia's amulet shaped like a silver locket. I rarely took it off.

"These don't travel through time, but we're both capable of that ourselves," Brianna said, putting the jade disc onto Sophie's palm then putting the watch on its chain around her own neck.

"I guess the fact that neither of us sensed them here means they work?" Sophie said, watching the disc catch the light as she held it dangling from its chain.

"Maybe," Brianna said. "I did every test I could think of, but I don't know what a bunch of powerful witches are capable of, or how persistent they are with watching for us. But let's assume very persistent and keep this visit short."

"We need answers," I said.

"I agree, but I can't help thinking that the answers might not be there. They might be in 1966."

"And how do we get to 1966?"

"I have no idea," Brianna said.

"If it seems like we've got nothing to work with, we'll head straight back," Sophie said, putting on the necklace. "Let's grab a change of clothes and get going."

Not that any of us were looking to argue about making haste, especially as the smell of baking chocolate cake was thick in the air as we ran past the kitchen.

After reaching out and examining the time portal every day for months, actually doing the magic to step through, it felt very strange.

And yet so right. Like it was something I was supposed to do, a part of me I had neglected for far too long. I had to remind myself that our calling wasn't being time travelers; it was beings guardians of the portal.

Still, it felt like being home, if a bit colder than 2019.

"Do we go in?" Brianna asked.

"I can look from here," I said.

"Me too," Sophie said.

"Good," Brianna said. "It's creepy since we figured out we're over-lapping the students of this time when we're in there."

"You assume no one is standing in the orchard right now but us," Sophie said.

"I think we can safely assume that," Brianna said. "It's even colder here than back home."

"Take my hand," I said, peeling off my gloves and extending my hands to the others.

"What? Why?" Brianna asked.

"I want to see if you can see what I see," I said. "Save us some time."

"Oh, right," Brianna said, pulling off her own gloves and stuffing them in her pockets. Sophie did the same. Once they were in contact with me, and all of us had controlled our breathing, I shifted my awareness to the world of threads.

I knew what the school should look like here. If anything, I had examined it more extensively than I ever had the version in 2019. I had to force myself to make a thorough search for the scribble lines because everything else was so different.

At last, I blinked myself back into normality, and we all dropped our hands.

"Did you see?" I asked.

"It was all glowing," Brianna said. "So brightly, it was like it was pulsing. Does it always look like that?"

"No," Sophie said before I could answer. "That was recent. I could sense it. It's new."

"New, and full of power," I said. "It always has a glow, because of all of the protection spells Miss Zenobia has cast over it and everything the students have done. But this is different. That pulsing, and the intense brightness. Someone has been doing a lot of powerful magic here. And I'm pretty sure it was more than one someone."

"Maybe we're jumping to conclusions," Sophie said. "I didn't sense what we had trapped in the glass sphere anywhere around here."

"Nor I," I said. "But someone's done something. What else could have changed?"

"It *is* a magic school," Sophie said.

"Not quite," Brianna said. "I mean, it's not Hogwarts. Miss Zenobia took in tons and tons of students who were just normal girls looking to gain a little polish to their education."

"Charm," Sophie said with a smile.

"And then there were the exceptional ones," I pointed out.

"Yes, but even then, those weren't all witches," Brianna said.

"Weren't they? I thought that's what she meant," I said.

"Not always," Brianna said. "Miss Zenobia used that in her notes for any girl who had more potential than a life as a wife and mother was going to satisfy."

"Like Cynthia Thomas," Sophie said, nodding as she put it together. "Meant to be a lawyer."

"Others became doctors or journalists or even spies in World War I," Brianna said.

"How do you know all this stuff?" I asked.

Brianna flushed red. "Sometimes, I need a break from my reading research, so I read some of the other things in the library."

"Which still sound to me like research," I said. "But I guess they're all in English."

"Do we know how many were witches, or at least how many witches were here in 1928?" Sophie asked.

"No," Brianna said. "She was always very careful not to name them in her notes. I think she was always afraid of witch hunts. She lived through a few."

"There must be something somewhere," I said. "Some super-secret journal or something?"

"She has a lot of hiding places all over the house," Brianna admitted. "Some of the boxes and cupboards have different contents depending on when during the moon phase you open them. Well, the moon and... you know."

"Not really, but please don't try to explain string theory to me again just now," I said. "I'm still trying to figure out spells that work with tripwires. We can clearly see a spell has been cast here, a big one. But there's no sign of what was in our heads. So does that mean that wasn't the purpose of the spell?"

"Not necessarily," Brianna said. "Like I said, the spell needed a trigger. But witches as powerful as these cast spells in layers. The bomb, the tripwire, then a ton of wards to keep it all out of our sight."

"So what can we do?" I asked. We all fell silent as each of us mulled that over. It was me who spoke first again. "I could look for objects outside of time," I said. "Like the wardrobe or the Mina Fox's crystal ball. That would be just the sort of thing you'd use for this purpose, right?"

Sophie was nodding along eagerly, but Brianna shook her head.

"No, that would be just what you wouldn't use here," she said.

"I don't know, Bree. It makes sense," Sophie said.

"No, it doesn't. Look at this house. How different is it, inside or out, between now and 2019? Most of the furniture is even the same. There would be no need to craft something that was outside of the normal flow of time. If you could use any mundane object at all, and be pretty confident it will still be here in 91 years, why would you bother with some rare magical item that would just draw attention to itself?"

I sighed. I was pretty sure she was right.

"So it really can be anything," Sophie said. "It could've been a door we all walked through, or a drawer we opened. Or a book."

"I think we've done all we can here," Brianna said. "We should get back before we're noticed."

"Not quite yet," I said. "Let's just walk around the house one time. Maybe whoever did this left a trail of some kind when they left."

"I don't know," Brianna said.

"We should be sure," Sophie said.

"All right," Brianna agreed, but she pulled out her wand before she started walking through the snow.

I missed my 2019 boots. At least my socks were warm.

We walked around the side of the house next to what was still a home without occupants in our time, currently the residence of a man who was a curmudgeon but also a bit of a shut-in. If he was watching us from the windows, he didn't bother us at all.

The traffic on Summit Avenue was busy, it being nearly dinner-time and Valentine's Day dinner at that.

As we came around the corner of the house to the garden path that ran parallel to Coco's house, I could see the orchard and where we had started from, and I had to admit there was no sign of a trail, magical or otherwise. Bunny tracks marked the snow around the bushes near the back porch, but nothing more sinister than that.

Then I heard someone call my name.

"Crap, that's Edward," I said without turning around. "Let's go."

"He's on the other side of the road," Sophie said, looking behind us. "Lots of traffic. Give him a minute."

"No, let's just go," I said.

"You should talk to him at least," Sophie said. "That would be the polite thing to do. Or, dare I say, charming?"

"Sophie, I don't even know what I would say to him after not seeing him since the New Year's Eve party when his fiancée died," I hissed. "And now it's Valentine's Day, which makes it all so much more awkward."

"And we're in the middle of an investigation, and possibly in danger," Brianna added.

"But it's Edward," Sophie said cajolingly.

"Seriously?" I shot back. "You've been dodging Antoine for months and months, and you're hitting me with this? Antoine, who seemed like the sweetest guy ever and clearly cares about you. Antoine, whom we have no reason to suspect is actually in any danger at all."

Sophie looked like I had just slapped her. I kind of felt like I had. But I wasn't going to take it back.

"If they are watching us now, and they see us talking to Edward-" Brianna said.

"You're right," Sophie said. "You're both right. I'm sorry."

"Let's just go before he gets across that street," I said.

We scurried towards the orchard. 1928 boots didn't have anything like the traction of my 2019 boots. Brianna skated along beside me. Sophie turned back only for a moment, gesturing with her wand at the oak tree that stood outside the dining room window.

There was a hiss and rush of falling snow, and then Edward yelping as it all crashed down on him.

"Is he all right?" I asked, turning back to see, but Sophie grabbed my arm and pulled me back around.

"He's fine," she said. "It's powdery snow. He'll dig himself out."

And then we were back in 2019, and I hadn't even gotten the one thing I had wanted out of 1928: a single glimpse of Edward.

But I had heard his voice saying my name. Saying my name with genuine excitement. For however brief of a moment, he had been happy to see me.

As much as I wanted it to be, it wasn't quite enough.

CHAPTER 8

r. Trevor's special Valentine's Day dinner was waiting
for us when we came in the door and made a welcome
distraction to our lack of progress on the investigation. He had done
far more than just made lava cakes. There was baked chicken with
creamy rice and asparagus drizzled in a buttery lemon sauce that was
so filling I feared I'd have no room for dessert.

But when he brought out homemade whipped cream and fresh
raspberries, I decided I could make the room. I slid my fork into the
side of my lava cake and watched the chocolate ooze over the raspberries.

"This is perfection, Mr. Trevor," Sophie said with her mouth full.

"Really?" Mr. Trevor said with a raised eyebrow. "I didn't think I
could top a surprise visit from an old friend bearing beignets."

"Those were good too," I said.

"It's going to be salads for a week after this," Sophie said glumly,
then took another bite. "So worth it, though."

"We'll handle the dishes, Mr. Trevor," I said. "We have some things
to go over; it will help to keep our hands busy."

"If you're sure," he said, and when we all insisted he said good night
and headed up the back stairs.

"Antoine would have liked this," Sophie said, pushing a raspberry through the last streak of chocolate on her plate. "He has a weakness for rich foods."

"You could've asked him to stay," Brianna said.

"No," Sophie said. "Not until I understand why I feel like I can't, anyway."

Brianna looked confused.

"Sophie has a compulsion," I said. "It might be part of the spell we haven't figured out yet or something else. But she feels like he has to stay away."

"It feels magical?" Brianna asked.

Sophie shrugged. "I don't know. I'm not sensing anything, but it's just such a strong feeling."

"Maybe if we figure out more about the spell that smothered our memories, we'll figure out that too," I said.

"Maybe," Sophie said, still pushing that same raspberry around her plate. Then she set down her fork without eating it. "I'm sorry I was teasing you before. I shouldn't do that."

"I know you're not trying to be mean or anything," I said.

"I do it a lot," Sophie said. "And I think it has something to do with being here without Antoine, and that's really messed up. It's not like it even makes me feel better or anything. I promise I won't do it again."

"I appreciate that," I said. "Things with Edward are complicated enough, you know? It's not like I can explain to him why I disappeared for months and why I just ran away from him. And even if we take care of this situation with Evanora and her coven, I don't see any way to have a real relationship across time."

"Cynthia did it," Brianna said. "Her entire life, she kept that up."

"She didn't have kids though," I said. "Can you imagine how impossible it would be to have kids in that situation?"

"Do you want kids?" Sophie asked.

"I don't know. I don't want to rule it out, though."

"Our duty is to guard the time portal, but that doesn't mean you have to guard it from this end," Sophie said.

"I think it would be weird to try to live there, in that version of the school where all the students are not quite there," I said. "I think it would drive me crazy."

"There might be other options," Sophie said.

"We should really focus on the Evanora situation first," I said.

"Of course," Sophie said. "I'm just saying, at some point, we're going to have to figure out a work/life balance, or we'll all go crazy."

"I have a balance," Brianna said as she got up and started gathering plates to carry into the kitchen.

"You think you do?" Sophie asked. "From the outside, it looks like you're all piled on the work side."

"Maybe what I think of as my life looks like work to you because it's not the sort of thing you enjoy, but I assure you I feel perfectly balanced," Brianna said.

I wanted to argue, but then I had to admit to myself that Brianna always seemed content. I don't know when she ever slept, but it never seemed to bother her.

"But don't you get lonely?" Sophie asked.

Brianna shrugged. "I was never really a dating person. It always felt like such a contrived activity. Most people don't enjoy the things I enjoy, and it's hard to discuss the really interesting things with them. I do love my cats, though."

"Not enough to give them names," Sophie teased.

"They don't need names to tell me who they are," Brianna said, taking her stack of plates into the kitchen. Sophie and I followed, she with the last of the chicken and rice and I with the other serving dishes.

"Well, names are helpful to the rest of us," Sophie said.

"Then it's a good thing you two named them," Brianna said. Then she turned on the sink, and the running water quieted our conversation as we put the leftovers into storage containers and cleaned up the dishes, table, counters, and stovetop before finally shutting off the water and drying our hands.

"What now?" Sophie asked, and we all knew she wasn't talking about more chores.

"Research," Brianna said. "The glow the school had in 1928 looked homogeneous, but I don't think it was. I think a lot of spells are layered there. I need to look some things up to get a better understanding, though. What are you thinking?"

"I think I'll search the whole house from top to bottom," Sophie said. "There are a lot of magical objects tucked away everywhere. I don't know what I'm looking for exactly, but I think I'll know it when I touch it. Or I'll come up empty," she said with a shrug.

"Are you hoping to find the trigger?" I asked.

"The spell would have long since dissipated," Brianna said.

"Maybe, maybe not," Sophie said. "Maybe there are other triggers for other spells. This is maddening, you know? That they can just keep laying traps in 1928 and we can just keep blundering into them 91 years later. I don't like it."

"Me neither," Brianna said. "Be careful. If you get any sort of sense of danger, wait until we're all together."

"Of course," Sophie said.

"What about you?" Brianna asked me.

"I'm not much use with your sort of research," I said to her.

"You could help me with the sweep of the house," Sophie said.

"I could, but I'm thinking I'll start with some research I *can* do," I said. "I want to head to the public library. I want to look up our mothers and the history of the area in 1966. Maybe I'll find some clues as to what happened here."

"What sort of clues?" Brianna asked.

"I don't know. Maybe nothing. But you've been all over this library. Is there any hint here as to what happened, why that was the last class when Miss Zenobia went on to live for another fifty years?"

"No," Brianna admitted. "I've always just assumed she got tired of teaching and retired. She was old."

"She was centuries old," Sophie said. "I agree with Amanda, something must have provoked that change. Something she didn't want to talk about after."

Brianna still looked skeptical.

"Look," I said. "Evanora and her group went to an awful lot of trouble to cloud our memories of our own mothers. Now we have them back, but none of us know a single thing that seems like a reason to take those memories away."

"Yes, what are they afraid we know?" Sophie agreed.

"Or are afraid we might find out," I said. "Sophie and I both came here in part with the hopes of digging up the past and finding answers. Clouding our memories stopped us from doing that."

"All right, I agree," Brianna said. "I'm just not sure the public library is going to help."

"Unless there are books here you haven't already paged through, I don't know where else to start," I said.

"Fair enough," she said.

"The library won't be open until morning, and I'm starting to feel a sugar crash coming on myself," Sophie said with a yawn. "I'll start the search in the morning after we finish the dawn ritual."

"Sounds like a plan," I said.

"I'm going to check a few things before I go to bed," Brianna said. "What time does the library close tomorrow?"

I looked it up on my phone. "Five," I said.

"Then as soon as you're home, we'll meet in our library and compare notes," Brianna said. "Oh, and remember what I said before about paying attention to your dreams. Memories could surface there that won't occur to our conscious minds. Keep a notebook by your bed and write down what you remember while it's still fresh."

"Great," Sophie said to me as we walked up the stairs to our bedrooms. "Tomorrow Brianna can comb through my usual anxiety dreams for hints of past events. That will be fun."

"No, the real fun will come when we get to my dreams," I said. "My dreams never make any sense. It'll probably be penguins ice skating to Rick Astley on an endless loop."

"Thanks for the earworm," Sophie said. "Like my anxiety dreams needed a soundtrack."

But when we gathered in the backyard at dawn and exchanged glances, we each just shook our heads. No dreams. No hints as to what we might remember that would be worth all of the effort Evanora and her witches had gone through to take it from us.

CHAPTER 9

*I*t was a good thing that the library allowed coffee in covered containers or I would've never made it through the many hours I spent combing through every issue of the local paper from 1966, then 1967. Then 1968.

If anything had happened with our mothers, it was long after that photograph had been taken. But I had no idea when. Since the library was only open until five, I decided not to break for lunch. Being hungry didn't exactly make me more patient as I scanned headline after headline.

I almost missed seeing my mother's name, but I really hadn't expected to see anything on the page of marriage announcements. There was no photo, just a little block of text to announce the imminent nuptials of Kathleen Stinson, no family listed, to a John Olgesen, son of Sven and Edith.

Olgesen? Not Clarke?

I took a picture of the computer screen with my phone and sent a copy of it to both Brianna and Sophie, noting the date of that paper was January 12, 1968. I took another swallow of coffee that was room temperature but still bitterly strong then continued scanning, eager for more breadcrumbs of information.

But I couldn't find any. There was no mention of my mother again under either Stinson or Olgesen, and no mention of Lula Collins or Marie DuBois.

And that marriage announcement didn't answer any questions. It just spawned a ton more questions.

The librarian had just announced they would be closing in five minutes when I finally found what might be another clue. It wasn't about our mothers specifically. It actually answered a different question I had been having for quite some time.

It was a picture of Coco's family's house, not burned down as I had been told, or at least not exactly. It looked more like something next to it had exploded, blowing in the entire side of the house closest to the charm school. I could see dark streaks of smoke damage on the crumbling stone walls, but it looked to me more like the kitchen had caught fire after whatever had happened to that wall.

And yet the charm school beside it was completely unharmed. The oak tree outside the dining room window didn't even look singed. What had happened? And on the Fourth of July of all days?

"Ma'am? We're closing now," one of the librarians said to me.

"Oh, right," I said. "Can I print this real quick?"

"This article?" she asked.

"Please," I said.

"I'll send it to the printer. You can grab it at the front desk. It looks like it'll be three pages. That's ten cents a page," she said.

"Cool. Thanks," I said, tossing my coffee cup into the trash and digging through the pouches on my backpack until I found a couple of quarters.

There was still one other patron in the library, watching the librarian behind the counter scan a monstrous stack of books that looked to be largely about trains. I queued up behind him, the quarters held tight in one hand as I looked at my phone with the other. No texts from the others. Had they seen mine?

"Amanda?"

I looked up to see the patron with the train books looking at me, and belatedly realized I was looking at Nick's grandfather.

"Mr. Larson," I said. "Good to see you."

Good, but mostly awkward. What had Nick told him exactly? Would he say we broke up? Were we ever actually dating?

"Good to see you too," he said. "No books?"

"No, I-" I started to say, but the librarian was waiting for me with paper in her hands. I handed her the quarters then took my change and thrust it in my pocket. "Just waiting for a printout, actually."

"Anything interesting?" he asked as we walked together towards the door where the other librarian was waiting, key in hand.

"Yes. Actually, it's about the house that used to stand on the property where your condo is now," I said, showing him the first page of the article. "Apparently there was some sort of explosion there on the Fourth of July in 1968."

"Strange, I always heard it was a fire," he said, squinting at the photo. "But that wall does look like something blew it in, doesn't it?"

"It was before your time, right?" I said.

"Well, I was around," he said, his eyes twinkling at me. "I lived in Minneapolis before I joined the army. After the war I lived in Wisconsin, because that's where my wife's people were. No, I didn't move to this area until after my wife died. That would've been 1977. There was a home on the lot at that time, but it was a shoddy build from a substandard contractor. Pretty much sank in on itself within a decade. Then came the condos." He tipped his head to one side. "You were asking about my neighbors before. Do you have a keen interest in local history?"

"Kind of," I waffled as we stepped out the second set of doors, out into the February evening.

Where I was promptly knocked back by an excited Irish setter.

"Finnegan!" I said, pushing his paws back down to the ground before giving him a scratch around the ears.

Then my eyes followed the leash to what I pretty much knew I would find on the other end.

"Hello, Amanda," Nick said.

"Hey," I said lamely. He was wearing a navy blue peacoat with a dark gray watch cap. His blond hair had gotten longer; I could see locks of it poking out from under the cap, twisted by the cold wind. He looked like he'd just come off the deck of a submarine after surveying the weather.

It was a good look for him.

"Finnegan and I shall head to the car," his grandfather announced, taking Finnegan's leash from Nick. "It was good to see you, Amanda. Hopefully, it won't be so long before we meet again."

"Yes," I said. My brain seemed incapable of producing more than that.

"You look good," Nick said to me, to which my response was something like, "ack."

I wished Sophie were there. I could really use a tree-load of snow dumped on top of me, swallowing me up. What was wrong with me?

"What was that?" Nick asked, the look in his eyes something between confused and amused.

"Thanks," I said, pulling myself together.

"You've got a glow to you," he said. Then, half teasing but also half serious, "is that a magic thing?"

"No," I said. Sophie might have that sort of magic, but it would never be my gift. "Maybe it's from the exercise. I got some weights for Christmas, and I've been lifting."

"Oh," he said, looking me over. But in my winter coat, there was no way he could tell if I had put on any muscle. "Does that help with the magic?"

"Actually, yes," I said. "I lift heavy. That takes a lot of focus and discipline. Breathing is very important. That translates to other things. But I'm sure you know that."

"Yes, I have a little experience with that," he said. "I confess I was getting a little worried. I hadn't seen you around in quite some time."

I felt my cheeks flush. He had been looking out for me? "Well, it's winter. I've mostly been indoors."

"But everything is going okay?" he asked. "You've not been in danger?"

"Nothing I couldn't handle," I said, which came really close to not being true.

"No more murders?"

"Not in this time," I said, and I knew he knew I was hedging every answer. He was about to ask me something else when a blast of car horn drowned him out. He turned, and we both looked to where his car was parked across the lot under one of the lights. His grandfather gave us an apologetic look as he corralled the Irish setter back into the back seat of the car.

"Finnegan is anxious to go," I said.

"Do you want a lift?" he asked.

"No," I said. "I have some thinking to do, and it's not so cold tonight, so I think I'll have a walk. Thank you, though."

"Of course," he said with a small smile. "See you."

"Yes, see you," I said. He turned and started walking towards the car. I slipped the backpack straps off my shoulders and dropped it at my feet, zipping it open to put the printout inside, then dropping the dimes back into a side pouch. But I was watching Nick out of the corner of my eye. I saw him look back at me no less than three times. Each time he saw me still watching him, seeing him looking back, and he'd give a little wave, and I'd wave back. I think by the time he got back to his car, we were both thoroughly embarrassed and yet each incapable of being the first one to leave.

But then he got into the car and pulled away with one last wave, and I was alone in the softly falling snow.

How often had he been thinking about me in the last few months anyway? Just how many times had he hoped to run into me on the sidewalk in front of our houses?

Was he finding a way to be cool with who I was and what I did?

I bit down on my own lip then thrust my hands into my coat pockets and started the walk home. I didn't want to be wondering such things. It felt like a betrayal of Edward.

And yet, hadn't I pretty much decided I could never be with Edward? And if I wasn't with Edward, why not be with Nick?

No, that didn't feel right. Somehow, it didn't feel fair to either of them. Edward wasn't so easily replaced as all that, and Nick didn't deserve to be thought of as a substitute for someone else.

They were both better off without me and all the trouble I brought with me. And I'd probably be better off with a nest of kittens like Brianna.

But unlike Brianna, I didn't think that'd be enough for me.

And maybe this relationship confusion was a family trait. Who was this John Olgesen my mother was married to in the 60s? And who was Clarke, he of no known first name, who had died by her side in the 90s? Had she loved one or the other or both?

Which one was my father?

It was a good thing I wasn't sharing the sidewalk with other pedestrians. The growling aloud I was doing in response to my own frustrating thoughts would be raising some alarms, I was sure.

Still, why was everything getting more complicated the more I tried to make it simple? It couldn't be this hard to decide what decade I wanted to live out my life in, and with which guy?

Okay, maybe it was kind of hard. I was pretty sure the intricacies of time travel gave anyone who meddled in it epic headaches.

No, Sophie had the right plan of attack. First, deal with this coven of witches who were somehow attacking us across decades of time then second, find a work/life balance.

Somehow, the second felt more impossible than the first.

CHAPTER 10

*W*hen I got to the library, I found Sophie already there with Brianna, waiting for me. Brianna had managed to clear enough space on one end of her massive table to accommodate a tray of tea and sandwiches. I must have just missed Mr. Trevor, as curls of steam were still rising up from the pile of sandwiches, and I could smell the roasted chicken from the night before making an encore appearance.

"Anything good?" Sophie asked as I slid into a chair unencumbered with stacks of Brianna's books. Brianna poured a cup of tea for me, but my attempts to reach for a sandwich were hampered by a small ball of fur lunging into my lap.

"Hey, Duke," I said, scratching around the white cat's over-sized ears. He purred loudly, closing his mismatched eyes in pleasure.

"Here," Brianna said, putting a plate with a couple of sandwiches in easy reach.

"Thanks," I said. "I did find a few things, but I'm not sure how helpful they are." I pulled the printouts out of my bag and explained about the marriage announcement and then the news story. Brianna examined the blurry newspaper photo then handed it to Sophie, who shifted the sleeping Ziggy from one shoulder to another before taking it.

"It doesn't tell us much," she said. "Something happened, and it looks like magic, but is it anything to do with our mothers or the time portal? It could be something else entirely."

"It gives us a date," I said. "But whether that date connects to anything else, who knows?"

"Data points are always good," Brianna said. "I'll add it to the time-line." She got up from the table, Jones trotting beside her as she brushed past the back of my chair. I saw something new in her little space: an old chalkboard, as big as a section of classroom chalkboard but on its own rolling frame. I couldn't quite see what was on it in the dim, mostly downward-directed light of the library, but when she wrote down the date from the newspaper, I could tell it was indeed a timeline.

"I'm going to make it a separate line," she decided, drawing another horizontal line across the board a few inches above the one that was already there.

"Separate timelines," I groaned. "That's always when time travel gets complicated, doesn't it?"

"It might not be separate," Brianna said. "In fact, I don't think it is. But that's just an intuition. I don't want to write it down as known fact when it isn't one, quite."

"Sure," Sophie said, then caught my eye and gave me a shrug and a smile. Neither of us was ever going to understand this stuff the way Brianna did. But if she thought such distinctions had a purpose, who were we to argue?

"I do wonder about the marriage announcement, though," I said. "Is this Olgesen my real father? Is he the one who died the day I was born, or was that someone else?"

"Maybe we can look into that more later," Sophie said. Brianna was still looking at the board as if hoping a pattern would emerge from the mostly blank space. Sophie went on, "you could get DNA testing done to find out, if you exhume the body. It could be this Olgesen guy was just wearing a shirt that said Clarke on it."

"Or it could be he stayed in the 60s when my mother jumped forward in time," I said. "If that's actually even what happened."

"I think that's the most likely explanation," Brianna said as she went back to her chair to take a sip of tea.

"Did you have a more fruitful day than me?" I asked.

Brianna sighed. "That depends on what you mean by fruitful. I might have uncovered too much information."

"What do you mean?" Sophie asked.

"I wanted to figure out what spells might have been done, starting with basic cloaking and warding spells," she said, pulling her little notebook out of her pocket. "I started by listing everything I thought I saw going on when we looked around in 1928. But I found way too many things that matched my observations. I think there might have been dozens of spells all layered and intertwined and covering each other up. Most of them wouldn't even have served any real purpose."

"Maybe the complexity was the purpose," I said. "They're trying to confuse you."

"Do they even know who I am?" Brianna said.

"What do you mean?" I asked.

"They know you. Evanora saw you with her own eyes, and they all were watching you on New Year's Eve. I think it's a safe bet they know your powers. Up until now I didn't think they were even really aware of Sophie or I. I mean, I would guess they knew you weren't alone, but did they know about our powers?"

"I assumed they did," I said.

"Why?" Sophie asked.

"They took all of our memories, right?" I said. "It seems like it would've been easier to just take mine if that was all that mattered to them."

"Can they see us here?" Sophie asked. "Can they be watching us now? Are they somewhere in the present world?"

We all looked around the gloomy corners of the library, as if we were going to see the shadowy forms of spies there. Something about the intensity of our mood set off the kittens, who all went charging away from us at once as if in response to a starter's pistol only they could hear.

"Ow," I protested, a row of red welts rising up from the skin of my forearm from where Duke had used it as a launch pad.

"If they could be here, there'd be no need for the time-delayed magic they've been using in 1928, would there?" Sophie asked.

"Well, if confusion is part of their plan," Brianna said with a shrug. "At any rate, I also spoke with Sephora in Boston. The coven that raised me is not so modern, but she can stop in and visit them in person for us. I loaded her up with questions about my mother, your mothers, and Miss Zenobia. I actually wrote up that timeline in the first place because it helped Sephora and I focus on the important bits."

"And what did they say?" I asked.

"I'll know tomorrow," Brianna said.

"Great. Waiting is my favorite," I said glumly.

"What about you, Sophie?" Brianna asked. "Did you find anything?"

"Just this," she said, and lifted a massive tome onto the table, where it landed with an echoing thud.

"What is that?" I asked as Brianna immediately started turning the pages.

"It's definitely full of magic," Sophie said. "Can't you feel it?"

I blinked into the world of threads, and the light coming from the book was blinding. I blinked back into the library.

"Definitely," I said. "But it's not out of time. The threads were connected to everything around us."

"It looks like a journal," Brianna said, pointing to headings on top of blocks of text. "See, these look like dates."

"Look like?" I asked, leaning forward. Then I saw what she meant. It did have the format of someone writing the day of the week followed by a month, day, and year. Only I couldn't read a bit of it. "What language is that?"

"What alphabet is that?" Sophie countered.

"It's some sort of code, I think," Brianna said. "But it's not the same code throughout the book. It keeps changing."

"How can you tell?" I asked.

"I'm scanning for patterns. Things like the year should be consistent, right? But if this is indeed a date, the symbols for the year is different each time. And I don't see a pattern to the change."

"So if you were going to decode it-" I started.

"I'd need to decode every section separately," Brianna said. "With all of the work that that implies."

My brain started to throb with a fatigue headache, just thinking about it, but Brianna sounded eager to dive into a particularly thorny problem.

"That's going to take time," Sophie said. "And it might not lead to anything. We don't even know what this is. It could just be some student's angsty journal from a totally different time period."

"Not with this kind of power," Brianna said, holding her hands spread before it as if warming them before a fire. "This has to be Miss Zenobia's work."

"So potentially important, but still maybe not," Sophie said. "Miss Zenobia lived for centuries. She probably filled a dozen tomes of that size before she even came to America."

"Can we carbon date it or something?" I asked.

"Maybe," Brianna said, and I could hear the gears in her mind spinning up to full speed.

"Hold on," Sophie said, putting her hands over the pages of the book as if that would stop Brianna. "Maybe that's not what we focus on first."

"What do we focus on first?" Brianna asked.

"The coven," I said, and Sophie nodded.

"You want to go looking for Evanora and the others?" Brianna asked, touching the little watch amulet she was still wearing around her neck.

"Not yet," I said. "But we need to learn more about them."

"How?" Brianna asked.

"I'm thinking two things," I said, leaning forward. "The first is just mundane, but might help. We get photos of all of them. Maybe someone in your circle of witches might recognize them. Maybe we already have their faces on the walls here, among all the class photos. Faces might give us names, and names could give us a sense of who they are and what they can do."

"How are we going to get photos?" Brianna asked, and I could see she was still nervous about physically hunting down a bunch of witches of unknown power.

"Otto," Sophie said, and now it was my turn to nod.

"He already knows them," I said. "Before New Year's Eve, they were letting him see them around, watching him. If he doesn't have photos of them already, it'll be simple for him to get them."

"Assuming they're still being visible like that," Brianna said.

"Assuming," I said with a shrug.

"It can't hurt to check," Sophie said.

"But that means going back to 1928," Brianna said.

"Yes, but we don't have to leave the school to contact him. And we don't have to hang around until he gets back to us. We can do just as before, only staying as long as we have to and then getting back home before those witches even know we're there," I said.

"Okay, so what's the second thing?" she asked.

"You told me once that few witches are generalists. Most focus on a particular kind of magic, right?" I asked.

"I'm about as close as it comes to a generalist," Brianna said. "But that's a matter of study, not practice. My actual magic tends to be verbal and short-range impact, or infused in objects."

"Okay," I said slowly, not entirely sure I grasped what she was saying. Energy bolts and amulets, I guessed. "But my magic is related to time, and Sophie does that wind thing when she dances."

"I'm working on Brianna's verbal and short-range impact stuff too," Sophie said, tapping the wand nestled against her forearm.

"I'm not following you," Brianna said. "What do you want to do?"

"Look at the spells," I said. "You said they were all intertwined and layered and meant to confuse you. It all looked like a blast of power to me too. It was overwhelming. But what if we tuned out the big picture and just started picking those spells apart?"

"Most of them were random distractors, I'm sure," Brianna said.

CHARM HIS PANTS OFF

"But even that might tell us something," I said.

"We'll observe their details when we dismantle them," Sophie said. "Catalog them. Look for patterns."

"Oh," Brianna said. "That might help. Even minor spells meant to be a distraction could tell us a thing or two about the witch. What she thinks is minor, how she manifests it. Yes, this could be very interesting."

"So we're agreed, then?" Sophie said, and she and I both got to her feet to join Brianna, who had never sat back down after consulting the chalkboard.

"Yes," Brianna said. "It's back to 1928. But promise me we're not leaving the school grounds."

"Not until we know what we're facing," I agreed.

"We need more intel before we go looking for a fight," Sophie said. Brianna looked at us both, chewing her lip in a worried sort of way. I could see a conflict starting to form between us. Sophie and I were going to be ready for a fight long before Brianna was done gathering intel.

That might become a problem later, but not yet. In this moment, we all agreed what needed to be done next.

We went back to 1928.

CHAPTER 11

When we came in through the back door in 1928 Brianna headed straight up the stairs to the library to set up the spell circle, but Sophie and I stayed behind in the kitchen, looking at the very old-fashioned phone on the wall near the butler's pantry.

"I know how to use a rotatory dial," Sophie said. "I even get that you hold that bit to your ear and talk into that bit megaphone bit there. But you know what I forgot?"

"That we don't have his number?" I said. "He named his club after you. There must be a directory around here somewhere."

"Would an illegal club be in the directory?" Sophie asked, raising an eyebrow.

"I see your point," I said. "A shame we can't just walk over. Would Brianna notice we sneaked off?"

"You know she would," Sophie said. "And she's right to be cautious."

"I guess," I agreed. I remembered every magical fight I'd already been in. I'd not yet faced anyone who was actually a witch, but what I'd nearly done on more than one occasion made me shiver just in the remembering. "Right, so what can we do from here?"

"A letter," Sophie said, catching at my sleeve. I followed her into the parlor where she went through the drawers of an incidental table until she found a fountain pen, a stack of stationary and an envelope.

"We don't have his address either," I pointed out.

"We don't need it," she said. "Think about it, we never see them because of that protective time spell thing, but this place is full of students. Most just normal young ladies, but a few witches like us, right?"

"Maybe," I said. "Were there always witches? I would think they'd be rare."

"Well, even if there weren't, someone around knows about their existence. Miss Zenobia herself must be around at least some of the time, right? She's the teacher."

"So what are you thinking?" I asked.

"We just leave this envelope out with his name on the front and a little note. 'Please deliver' or something like that. Once we walk out of the room, it becomes a thing that they can see too, right?"

"I don't know," I admitted. "It's certainly worth a try. If that doesn't work, there's always running next door and getting Coco to help. But I'd rather leave her out of it."

"No, we want her out of harm's way as much as possible," Sophie agreed. I knew we were both picturing the newspaper photo of her house, half reduced to rubble by something blowing out from the charm school. Did she still live there in the 60s? She'd be a middle-aged woman, but it wasn't inconceivable.

"What are you saying to him?" I asked as Sophie wrote in her elegant script. Even bent over from a standing position her writing was perfectly formed.

"To gather everything he knows, photos if possible, and bring it here to the school," she said, talking and writing at the same time.

"And how will we know he did it?" I asked.

"Stuff gets forwarded to us through time all the time," Sophie said. "Like our invite to the New Year's Eve party. The students or perhaps Miss Zenobia herself in 1928 just put it in a cubby, and when Mr. Trevor lays out the morning papers, he also sets out that mail. It has dates."

"And he has all of this in his office?" I asked. "Why don't we just take everything and read through it all now? Some of it might be important."

"We could ask him," Sophie said. "I'm not sure it would make much sense with no context."

"But some of it could be useful," I said.

"Maybe," Sophie said. "I just keep thinking of what Brianna said. Light touch with this time travel stuff. Maybe when you understand your power better, we'll know what's safe to meddle with."

"Maybe," I said. Brianna's warnings were why I had never done even the most basic research, like whether Coco really did still live in her childhood home in the 60s. Or what happened to Edward after 1928.

Brianna's warnings didn't come with a terribly specific idea of what would happen, just a general sense that it was better not to know. No, the real reason I hadn't looked was because I was afraid. I couldn't think of a single fate that wouldn't upset me to read about it. That he died young, perhaps even because of something I had done with my magic? That he remained a bachelor for all of his days, pining for a certain witch who never appeared again in 1928? That he grew old and died surrounded by generations of loving family he had with someone else?

Yeah, there were no happy endings for me in this one. But I was very sure the moment I gave in and started looking stuff up, that would be the ending for me. My part in the story would stop with that act.

Sophie left the envelope and the note on the incidental table in plain view of anyone heading towards the front door, then went upstairs to join Brianna in the library.

"Ready?" I asked.

"Yes," Brianna said. "This is going to be exhausting."

"I'm sure you're up for it," I said.

"No, it's going to be exhausting for the two of you," she clarified. "I know what to do to pull the spells apart, and I'll keep a mental catalog until we're done and I can write it all down. But in the meantime, I'm going to need power. So much power, a constant supply. That's where you two come in."

"It sounds like a little tweak to what we usually do," Sophie said. "We flow power through each other all the time. This is just hitting pause at the moment where you are the focal point."

"Yes, exactly," Brianna said. "But I will actually be draining you, both of you. We should have a signal, if it all gets to be too much."

"I think collapsing on the floor is a pretty good signal," Sophie said. "We've got this Bree."

"Just be careful with the brainstorming thoughts," I said.

"I will," she promised. "I'll need all my focus on what I'm doing."

We sat together in a circle on the floor, pretty much in the same spot where we'd removed the brain fog from our own minds in 2019. I controlled my breath, shifted my awareness, then expanded it until I could feel Sophie and Brianna on either side of me. Their magic was like a pulsing glow, warm and familiar.

Sophie's hands began to dance, and I saw her catching and pulling little threads of light, gathering them up and feeding them into Brianna, then attracting more with her graceful movements.

My own methods were a lot more blunt, but I slowed my motions down, careful not to burn Brianna with power.

I could see the clockworks of her own power around her as she began to speak arcane words, her wand summoning the first of many spells from the walls of the house to the center of our circle where she poked at it, never ceasing her chanting, until the tight knotwork of the spell unraveled and the threads broke away, the light within them dying as they drifted off to the far corners of the library.

As we worked, I tried to see if I could tell what the spells were. Some I could see were time spells from the way they pulled the threads of magic into elaborate braids that just made sense to my eyes. But most were more like the brain fog spell, just angry squiggles of power that had no order to my eyes, no story I could tell.

We worked for hours. Occasionally I would sense Sophie's energy beginning to flag, and I would catch up a ball of magical light and pass it to her. I don't know if she was aware, but each time her back would straighten, and her hands would become more fully expressive as they teased the threads into dancing through her fingers.

But even I couldn't keep it up forever. I was narrowing my focus to just gathering the energy and feeding it to Brianna. I wasn't trying to watch the spells as she dismantled them anymore. I certainly wasn't paying attention to the world outside of the three of us.

So it came as a bit of a surprise when Brianna untangled one last particularly brutal knot of magic, and there was no spell to pull into our circle after it.

We all opened our eyes. "Is that it? Did we get everything?" I asked, but Brianna just held up a finger to ask for silence.

Sophie and I watched her scribble away inside her notebook, filling page after page at a furious pace. She even had to switch pens at one point as the first ran dry.

By the time she was done, it was well past midnight, but her eyes were bright with energy. Maybe we'd given her too much. There'd be no sleep for her now.

"Did we get it all?" Sophie asked her. Brianna tipped her head then gave a qualified nod.

"Everything else around us felt like older magic," Brianna said. "I didn't want to risk damaging the spells Miss Zenobia wove into the house itself. We need that protection, all of us over all of the decades of the school." Then she launched herself to her feet, putting out a hand to help each of us get our own weary legs under us.

"Now what?" Sophie asked, but Brianna just pulled us along, out of the library to the door of Miss Zenobia's office. She dropped our hands as she looked around. By square footage, it should have been a rather spacious office. But long decades of acquiring magical objects had crowded it full of more things than I could even name. I did recognize a few things we had managed to destroy in the present, releasing spells I wasn't anxious to tangle with at the moment. I hugged my arms close to my sides and stayed in the doorway.

"Ah!" Brianna cried, running around the desk and standing on tiptoe to reach something on the top of the shelf behind the desk chair.

The box she set on the desktop was very, very familiar. The last time I had been in this office with that box was the night I had seen the ghostly form of Miss Zenobia Weekes. The night I had found out I was a witch.

"Should you be touching that?" Sophie asked. She, like me, had opted to stay close to the door.

Brianna ignored that question, but she did seem to change her mind about lifting the latch to open the lid. "This was the focal point of the real spells," she said.

"Wait, are you saying everything was a lie?" I asked.

"What? No!" Brianna said. "I told you, Miss Zenobia's spells have a very different feel to them than anything this coven whipped together. And what Miss Zenobia did, to send a piece of herself into the future to speak to us on that night, that was very advanced magic. No one in that coven is remotely at that level. And it had a cost. Years of her life, remember?"

"You're sure?" I said.

"Absolutely," she said.

"But Miss Zenobia cast that spell just last year before she died, right?" Sophie said. "So right now, that box is empty. Right?"

We all looked at it, but none of us wanted to test that theory.

I blinked to shift my awareness to the world of threads.

The box was there on the desktop, between Brianna and me. It was like a black hole of power, glowing darkly as it pulled light in to collapse on itself, the threads around it all warping to give it a wide berth.

I opened my eyes. "It's an object out of time," I said. "Like Mina Fox's crystal ball. I thought that happened because it was ineptly made?"

"I thought so too," Brianna said. "Brute power. Maybe what you're seeing is just the form of the box now, in 1928. Decades before Miss Zenobia puts it to another use."

"There must have been a reason she chose it," Sophie said. "Some property that suited her spell."

"And it was the focal point of the coven's spells too?" I asked.

"Yes," Brianna said. "When the box opened at the appointed hour to release that sequestered piece of Miss Zenobia so she could speak with us for those few minutes, it also triggered the memory-erasing spell. Somehow, the coven knows what this box is and that we'll all be close to it at the same moment."

"But how did Miss Zenobia never see their magic contaminating it?" I asked.

"Because we just removed it all?" Sophie suggested.

I threw up my hands. "If we removed it all, then how did we lose our memories?"

"I dismantled that spell as well," Brianna said. "It was the last, toughest one."

"So we never lost our memories at all? Only we did?" I said.

"We remember that happening," Brianna said. "It doesn't mean it did."

"Huh?" Sophie said.

"Memories are weird," Brianna said. "Every time you access a memory, you risk altering it."

"Maybe it's too late at night to discuss memory magic," Sophie said, rubbing at her temples. "Or too early in the morning."

"I wasn't talking about magic," Brianna said. "That's science. It's very interesting actually-"

Sophie put up a hand to halt the flow of what was certainly going to be far too much information. "Too late. Too early. Too tired."

"We should get back to our own time," Brianna agreed.

"Do we take the box with us? Or do we not because we didn't before? Or does it even matter?" I asked tiredly.

"Leave it," Brianna said, but then took out her wand. "I'll ward it first, just to be on the safe side. It'll just take a moment."

Sophie and I left her to it, making our way one slow step at a time down the stairs.

"She's going to be up all night, isn't she?" Sophie said. "And I'm dead on my feet."

"We maybe gave her too much and didn't keep enough for ourselves," I said.

"Says you," Sophie softly scoffed. "I felt you giving me extra. Don't you ever run out?"

"The world seems to hold a lot of power I can access with a touch," I said. "It's kind of scary."

We heard the sound of Brianna coming out of Miss Zenobia's office, her feet running down the corridor to the stairs, and we paused outside of the parlor to see the letter and note we'd left there now gone.

"I guess your plan worked," I said.

What did the students of this era think of us, though? How far into the future did the school exist, anyway?

The thought made a shiver run up my spine. The time bridge hadn't existed forever. It had begun at some date, and it would have to end at some date. It wasn't always going to exist. Somehow knowing that didn't feel like knowing that someday our sun was going to go supernova or whatever. It felt a lot more immediate than that.

Like it was all going to come to an end soon. I was never going to live long enough to see the Earth's sun go cold and dark, but in that moment I was sure I was going to see that time bridge collapse. I could feel it in my bones.

It was not a comfortable feeling.

CHAPTER 12

"*A*manda! Amanda, wake up!"

My eyes weren't open yet, but I had the distinct feeling that Brianna had been saying my name and shaking my shoulder for quite some time. I peered up at her through the narrowest crack between my lashes.

"It's too early," I told her.

"It's nearly noon," she said.

"Noon!" In an instant, I was wide awake, sitting up and reaching for my clothes. "The bridge-"

"It's all right," Brianna said. "I checked all of the wards and everything on my own. You and Sophie needed the rest."

"Is Sophie up yet?" I asked.

"I'm getting her next," Brianna said. "I found a spell I think might help us make sense of that journal."

"A decoding spell?" I asked as I pulled on my jeans.

"Better," Brianna said and gave me a wide grin. "Get some coffee and food in you and meet me in the library."

I finished dressing and headed down the back stairs to find Sophie already in the kitchen, putting a mug of cold coffee into the microwave. She waited for me to pour one of my own before shutting the door and pushing the too-loud buttons.

"Toast?" I said as I headed over to the breadbox.

"Please," Sophie said, or mostly said before an enormous yawn interrupted her. Then a curious look passed over her eyes.

"What is it?" I asked.

"I'm not sure," she said. "Brianna woke me up too fast. But I think I was dreaming about my mother."

"She wanted us to write that down," I said. "What did you dream?"

"That's just it; it's all gone now," she said. "I think we were dancing together."

"Magical dancing?" I asked. Sophie shook her head.

"We were dancing to Salt N Peppa," Sophie said. "It was on the radio."

"That sounds like a memory," I said.

"But not a helpful one," Sophie said, quickly pulling the door of the microwave open before the beep could sound.

"Maybe if you think about it again before you go to sleep tonight, you can finish the dream," I said.

"I'll try that," she said.

Brianna was waiting for us in the library, practically bouncing on her toes in impatience. There seemed to be more open books sprawled about than usual, which was saying something.

"I hope this isn't going to require too much energy, because I just don't have it," Sophie said, slumping into a chair with her mug of coffee and slice of buttered toast.

"Actually the spell I have in mind calls on Amanda's particular talents," Brianna said. "Are you up for it?"

"I don't know," I admitted. "I don't know the first thing about code breaking. What would you need me to do?"

"I found this," she said, picking out one of the open books and glancing at it before shoving it into my hands. "Does that look like something you can do?"

It took me a moment to realize that what I was looking at was meant to be a sketched version of the world as a web of threads, as I saw it when I summoned my power. Not that I could draw it any better myself. I wouldn't even want to try. A picture may be worth a thousand words, but that world is far too information-dense to be contained on a two-dimensional page no matter how intricate the drawing.

I continued to study it as I finished my toast then licked the last of the butter from my fingertips. Then I glanced at the text. It wasn't in English.

"Can you read this?" I asked.

"Some," Brianna said. "It's an older version of Italian, but not quite Latin, and the writer seems to have been a lover of contemporary slang. It would be like someone from centuries in the future trying to listen to modern teenagers at the mall conversing with each other. I can get the gist."

"What is it?" Sophie asked, leaning across the table to look at the illustration in the book, upside-down from her point of view, but I wasn't sure that mattered.

"Amanda said her power isn't so much time as story, right?" Brianna said, bouncing on her toes as her excitement got the better of her again.

"A sequence in time of relationships between things," I said. "If I examine things closely enough, I guess they tell me stories. You think that will work with this book?"

"I don't just want you to examine it," she said, sitting on the edge of my chair, so she put her own finger on the page and trace a pattern in the web of lines. "This is a way of teasing out that entire story and giving it a magical form."

"Oh," I said, watching her finger move through the drawing.

"Someone writing in a journal, they are creating a sequence through time, right? And they add to it over time. That's totally your thing," Brianna said.

"I guess," I said, but I wasn't sure.

"I don't think this would work with any old journal," Brianna said. "It's only because this is probably Miss Zenobia's work, right? That or another witch, but I'm really thinking Miss Zenobia. She wrote this for a reason."

"She put it in code for a reason," Sophie said.

"That's to keep out the nonmagical types," Brianna said. "She wants us to read it. She put herself into it as she recorded just the things she wanted to record."

"It sounds like you're talking about what she did with that box," Sophie said.

"This is different," Brianna said. "That was a piece of her own self, set aside at great sacrifice. This will be limited to just what's within the journal. The version of herself contained in this book might not even be aware she's Miss Zenobia. But once you manifest her, she can answer any question we put to her, provided that the answer is somewhere in this book."

"Neat," Sophie said. "Also, I'm never keeping a journal."

"I've never tried anything like this," I said. "And my wand is still not my wand."

"We're going to work together," Brianna said. "I'll direct the spell with my own wand. I just need to see through your eyes. Sophie should be in our circle but just to balance us out."

"I can do that," Sophie said, and she did look a little better now that she had some caffeine coursing through her veins.

"All right," I said.

We sat down in a circle and put the book between us, open to the first page. I took several slow breaths then shifted to the world of threads to look at the book.

It was still glowing brightly, but as I looked deeper, I saw there was something dwelling within it. It didn't look like a spirit or a ghost or anything. I had looked inside of so many people since I had discovered my power I knew what consciousness looked like. This wasn't that.

But it was something.

I sensed Brianna waiting, wand raised, and I willed my perceptions over to her. Her breath caught with wonder, but she quickly brought her mind back to the task and began chanting and drawing the thing out of the book with little flicks of her wand.

And suddenly we were all sitting on the floor looking up at the ghostly form of Miss Zenobia Weekes. She looked younger, far younger than I would have expected. I had assumed that if she had lived for centuries, she had probably looked like she did at the end for decades, but perhaps that wasn't the case.

But Brianna was frowning, and that made me nervous.

"Do you know who you are?" Brianna asked the form.

"Oh," the form said as if startled to be spoken to. "My name is... Z?" she said uncertainly.

"And do you know what year it is?" Brianna asked.

I thought for a moment, that question would confuse the journal ghost. Wouldn't she remember every year all overlapped, since she embodied them all?

But then I remembered that we had pulled out a sequential memory. A story with a beginning and end.

"It was 1968 the last I recall," Z said. She was floating several inches off the floor, and the book under her hem began to rustle, the pages turning until it got to the very end. The last entry ended halfway down the lefthand page, and the righthand page was blank. "Yes, I remember now. 1968."

"What do you remember first?" I asked.

"Coming to St. Paul, Minnesota," she said. "Not much here at the time. Not a bit like home."

"And where was home?" I asked.

"I don't know," Z said, almost merry in her lack of knowledge. "I don't think I ever wrote that bit down. Just that this place is not like home."

"That's all right," Brianna said. "We're mostly interested in the last things you know. They should be freshest in your memory."

"I don't know about that," Z said with a frown. "I think some of the middle bits are clearer. Towards the end, the writing gets a little irregular."

"It might be worth taking the time to decode it all later," Brianna said under her breath, and I was pretty sure she was talking to herself. Then she looked back up at Z. "What can you tell us of the last class?"

"The last class?" Z said. "You say that with such finality. Aren't you students too?"

"Please answer the question," Brianna said. Z frowned. There was enough Miss Zenobia in her to not like being given orders.

But she was a summoned form, conjured up to answer questions. She tapped her phantom fingertips together as she considered. "Not as many students as in years gone by. No, not much call for charm schools, especially not little local ones like mine. But there is always a need to educate witches, and I had six here at the time."

"Six?" Sophie said. "Not three?"

"Six is three and three," Z said. At first, I thought she was being sarcastic, but then she continued on. "Three were very tight, very focused on working magic together. Ooh, they had such potential. But the other three? Well, they couldn't much be bothered."

"Names, please?" Brianna said.

"Oh dear, I'm afraid it's just first names for me," Z said. Which was a relief; I was expecting it to be initials all the way through.

"Who were the three who did the magic?" Brianna asked, then glanced at Sophie and then at me.

"Patricia was their leader. Such a diligent student, always so eager to learn. Linda and Debra were fine in their own ways, of course, but without Patricia I'm not sure how much they would've accomplished. It's always lovely as a teacher to have a student like that, one that motivates the others. The whole class achieves more than you could ever imagine."

"The whole class? Did she inspire the other three as well?" Brianna asked. If she was disappointed that our mothers weren't named as the three best students, she didn't show it.

"She did at first," Z said. "When they were all younger, and magic was more like a game. It was only when I started to show them the whole world and what was in it that the others started to pull away. Patricia was driven to know it all, to face things as they were. She managed to keep Linda and Debra close by her sides, but the others were drifting away."

"Marie wanted to dance," Sophie said.

"Yes, and she was so talented," Z said with a smile.

"And Kathleen?" I asked. "She got married?"

"Married, but still a student," Z said. "She was loyal, if not so driven as Patricia. Patricia striving for new heights might have put her off, I sometimes think. The two always butted heads, but Kathleen hated competing. She'd rather leave the game and let Patricia declare herself the winner then to fight for her position. Pity. She had talent, but she chose to waste it."

I could feel my cheeks burning and reminded myself that Miss Zenobia, for all her power, was just one woman. This was just one woman's opinion. It didn't sum up all that was my mother, not by a longshot.

"And Lula?" Brianna asked. "She never lost interest in magic, did she?"

"Well, her interest in magic was never about using it for anything," Z said. "Just to study the history. Or rather, she was always planning all of the stops on an epic tour of the old countries that she never quite was ready to undertake. Or maybe she did! I don't know what happened after it all fell apart."

"What all fell apart?" we all asked at once, sitting up straighter.

"Well, everything," Z said, surprised at the looks on our faces. "But most specifically, the time portal itself."

CHAPTER 13

*W*e all started asking questions at once, Brianna managing two or three to Sophie and mine's one each, but it didn't matter since Z couldn't make sense of any of it.

"Children, children," she said, making settle-down gestures with her hands. "One at a time, please."

"Tell it all," I said. "From the beginning."

"Not the very beginning!" Brianna quickly interjected.

"Start with the time portal falling apart. Explain that," Sophie said.

Z looked thoughtful for a moment, as if accessing her memory like an old computer. I could almost hear the whir and whine of a hard drive booting up. Then she gave us an apologetic smile. "I don't contain all the answers."

"Just tell us what you do know," Brianna said. "We can take it from there."

"I was called away," Z said. "I don't know by who, to where, or for what purpose. I just know I wasn't here. There is a gap of about a week in my entries that lines up with that point."

"Are pages missing?" Brianna asked.

"No, nothing sinister," Z said. "My last entry is very rushed. I think I left out a lot because there simply wasn't time."

"Do you think you were called away deliberately?" I asked. "Like it was a distraction?"

"No," Z said after a moment's thought. "If that had been true, I would have noted it. I'm sure of that."

"So what happened while you were away?" Brianna asked.

"I had left my students in charge," Z said. "Kathleen was the oldest, but she was expecting a baby."

"Does that affect magic?" I asked.

"Yes, but in unpredictable ways," Brianna answered me. "One spell will fizzle, another will have ten times the effect. It varies by witch and by spell and by how far along she is and by time of day."

"Unpredictable," I said, nodding.

"Indeed, and so I asked her to rely on Patricia if anything should come up that she couldn't deal with," Z said. "There shouldn't have been any problems."

"The bridge across time was stable?" Brianna asked.

"What do you mean by stable?" Z asked.

"Well, after..." Brianna started to say, then quickly decided that 'you died' was a tactless thing to say. "After we arrived here, when the bridge had been untended for a time, there were weak points. Places where things could slip through. Gaps in the spells."

"Oh dear," Z said, putting her hands to her mouth. "No, that was just what I was afraid would happen. Oh, dear."

"So that was after all this happened?" Sophie asked.

"Yes. At the time I left, the time portal was as strong as Juno and I could make it. It extended from me to her, although her end tended to move through time. I never quite knew if she did that deliberately or if there was something else going on. Juno was the one with time powers, not me. I barely understood it. I felt sure she should be able to control it."

"You and Juno built it together?" Brianna asked.

"Yes. I was here, in my standard time. I never much cared for time travel, so my personal timeline is as close as possible to a straight line, day after day in succession."

"But not Juno," I guessed.

"Juno was always searching for... something. I never really understood her. Everything I did to get to her, working on my end with magic I could barely even do to reach out to her across time, and when I finally connected with her, she refused to come through."

"Why?" Brianna asked.

"I suppose she knew I was planning on stripping her of her power when she got here," Z said.

"What? Why?" I asked. "That sounds so extreme. She was your sister."

"She was making trouble again, I just knew it," Z said. "She meddled in time streams back home. That was what we fought about. It took decades to find her here after that fight. Read my pages; you'll see how sincere I was. I was sorry she had gotten lost in time. I devoted my entire life to getting her back. But once I found her, she chose to stay lost. I could keep a tether to her, but that was all."

"So the other end kept moving," Brianna said. "But the bridge itself was strong?"

"I could've gone to her at any time," Z said, "if that's what you're thinking. But I wanted her to come to me."

"How long did you wait?" Sophie asked.

"Decades," Z admitted. "It took so long to create in the first place; I couldn't give up on it. But by 1968, when I went to do whatever needed doing, it had been decades. Just waiting for Juno to admit she was wrong and come home so I could forgive her."

"Did your students know about any of this?" Brianna asked.

"The magical ones knew about the time portal," Z said. "Not about the family business."

"Did Juno destroy the bridge?" Brianna asked, but I was already shaking my head before Z answered.

"Oh, goodness, no. Juno was the bridge," Z said. "It exists because of her. I don't have time magic, but she has it like no other witch that ever was."

"So when you say you reached out to her, she was reaching back to you? She had to in order for this time portal spell to work?" Sophie guessed.

"Yes. But the moment her mind brushed mine, she knew what I was intending. She tried to flee, but she couldn't pull away from my timeline entirely. My magic was too powerful, and I would never let her go. But I wasn't going to go after her either."

"You couldn't?" Brianna asked, frowning skeptically.

"It was important that she come to me," Z said. "She was in the wrong. It was her place."

Sophie pressed a hand over her eyes, and I felt like doing the same. Everything came down to two siblings with a beef? For centuries?

"So what destroyed the bridge?" Brianna asked.

"I don't quite know," Z said. "I was away, far away, when it was attacked. My magic was part of it; I felt the effects when the spells started hitting it. But more than that, I heard Juno calling out to me across time. She was screaming for help. I used so much power getting to her I'm surprised I survived the experience."

"What spell?" Brianna asked.

Z shrugged apologetically. "I didn't write that bit down."

"What did you see when you got home?" Sophie asked.

"The part of the time bridge that was tethered to the orchard in the backyard was still attached, but only barely. And the other end was so unstable it was almost impossible to perceive. It jumped through centuries of time. Just trying to look at it nearly drove me mad. What it must have done for Juno, I cannot even say."

"And the students?" I asked.

"Oh, the students," Z said with a sigh. "It took days, no weeks, just to get things under control well enough for me to come back out of the time portal. And by that time there was no sign of any of them."

"They weren't around when you arrived?" Brianna asked.

"For the split second I was even aware of this house and its contents, no."

"But the house next door? Was it blown in?" I asked.

She shrugged. "If it were, I didn't write that down."

"And Juno?" I asked.

"I don't know," Z said. "I emerged from the time portal having managed to tether the far end in a specific time, but I heard nothing of

Juno. Her cries had gone silent before I made it home, and all of the weeks I spent within the portal showed no sign of her anywhere."

"What's the last thing you wrote?" Brianna asked.

"I had just spent a few days in bed recovering," Z said. "I was intending to go back into the portal to do more magical repair. Juno had to be in there somewhere. I thought perhaps she had been… scattered? Maybe I could bring her back together again? I'm sorry, I struggle with deciphering my own writing in the end here."

"Nice," I grumbled.

"What else?" Brianna asked.

"I was planning on bringing Cynthia Thomas across time," Z said. "She was a bright student. Not a witch, but capable of other things. I needed someone I could trust to manage the house while I worked in the place between times. If the government or someone tried to take my house while I was gone, the orchard would be in danger. I couldn't risk that."

"And you never looked for the students?" I asked.

"I was intending to, once the portal was more stable," Z said. Then she smiled brightly. "Perhaps there's a second volume."

"Perhaps," I said, but Sophie was shaking her head. She hadn't found one, and we both doubted one existed.

There was a reason there were never any more students in the school. Miss Zenobia had dedicated herself night and day to repairing the bridge across time that contained her sister.

And Juno had hidden from her. Or been hidden from her, although somehow I had never gotten a damsel in distress vibe off of her.

"One last question?" Brianna said.

"Yes, dear?" Z said, clasping her hands together.

"Explain this code to me," she said.

"Oh, it's perfectly simple, provided one is acquainted with the language of the Celts," Z said.

She went on from there, but I tuned her out. Honestly, it wasn't going to make any sense to me anyway.

95

CHAPTER 14

We ate an early dinner in gloomy silence, each lost in our own thoughts, only minimally responding to Mr. Trevor when he addressed us.

He wasn't offended. He knew when we were in problem solving/investigation mode. And the more I learned about Miss Zenobia and got a sense of what his years with her as his boss must have been like, the more his unbothered attitude began to make perfect sense.

If he were anyone besides who he was, he would've quit decades ago.

"Well? What are we thinking?" Sophie finally asked, folding her arms as she looked at each of us in turn.

"I feel like I know less now than I did before," I said. "What really happened in 1968? Miss Zenobia went far, far away, and something came from across time to attack her students?"

"Is that what we're thinking?" Brianna asked, blinking.

"What did you think?" I asked.

"I thought they were fighting each other," she said.

"What gave you that idea?" I asked.

"Three and three," Sophie said. "That's a weird way to say six."

"I don't think it was accidental either," Brianna said.

"I thought that just meant three determined witch students and three…"

"Slackers?" Sophie said.

"Come on, who doesn't lose the mission a little bit when they're eighteen or nineteen?" I asked.

I was asking the wrong people. They had both been working extremely hard on earning master's degrees while I was back in my hometown, doing the same job as always. I guess in my way; I'd never lost the mission either. I had simply been doing what that annoying compulsion had told me to do.

"I should talk to Juno," I said.

"No," Sophie and Brianna said at once.

"Why not?" I asked. "She can explain everything. She was there."

"And you would trust her version of events? She keeps offering you dark power," Sophie pointed out.

"She keeps offering me power," I amended. "The darkness I tend to find on my own."

"We'll keep it as an option of last resort, okay?" Brianna said. "We did get one lead we can work on."

"The three other students," Sophie agreed. "We only have first names."

"First names and a photograph with last names on the wall upstairs," I said.

We all looked at each other then got up from our chairs at once to race up the stairs to the wall outside Miss Zenobia's office.

Sophie got there first, taking the picture down from the wall and bringing it into the library where we could see it in better light.

"Do you recognize any of them?" she asked.

I looked at each of the faces in turn. They were all dressed like middle-class girls from 1968, if a bit more preppy than hippy. Patricia Dougherty had most of her blonde hair pulled back in a ponytail, the bangs getting tangled in the lashes of her blue eyes. Linda Sasse was shorter and rounder with dull brown hair, dark eyes, and freckles everywhere. Debra St. John reminded me a bit of a green-eyed

Morticia Addams, willowy tall with dark hair spilling loosely around her shoulders.

"No," I said. "But that's not surprising. I don't really see things in the threads in a photograph kind of way. It's more like I'd know then again if I met them. Their magic would feel familiar."

"I'm not sure how useful that will be," Sophie said. "Knowing who's killing you just before the spell hits."

"Let's not start with the dark thoughts," Brianna said. "We have their complete names now. That's a good thing."

"You think they'll be listed in the phonebook?" I asked.

"Maybe they're all dead," Sophie said. "Maybe whatever was after our mothers went after them too. We're really only guessing they weren't all on the same team."

"I'll start with Googling the names anyway," I said with a sigh and went over to the computer to switch it on.

"I'm going to call Sephora and see how it went with the Boston coven," Brianna said. "I'll see if the names mean anything to her."

"I'll check the school records," Sophie said. "Maybe there's something." But she didn't sound hopeful.

I was just about to sit down at the computer when I heard the chime of the doorbell.

"Who could that be?" I asked.

"Door to door salesmen?" Sophie said with a shrug.

"Maybe it's Antoine," I said.

"It isn't Antoine," Sophie said.

"You sound sure," I said.

"I am sure," Sophie said, showing me her phone, not close enough for me to read the texts themselves, just how many of the little colored bubbles there were when she scrolled through them.

"You've been keeping in touch," I said, wondering when she found the time. Hadn't we constantly been together?

"With Auntie Claire too," she said. "And it's not Auntie Claire downstairs either."

The doorbell chimed again.

"I'm on a call!" Brianna yelled from the back of the library.

"I'll get it," I said, and tromped down the stairs to pull open the heavy front door.

And found Nick just turning to leave. He spun back around as I swung the door open and I saw he had a manila folder in his gloved hands.

"Hey," he said.

"Hi, Nick," I said. "I wasn't expecting to see you again so soon."

"Can I come in? Just for a minute. I have something for you, but it's cold out here," he said.

"Sure," I said, stepping back so he could brush past me. He pulled off his hat and ran a hand through his hair but shook his head when I gestured towards the parlor.

"Better not in these boots, and they're a bear to lace up," he said. "I'll stay on the rug here. I just wanted to give you this." He thrust the manila folder at me.

"What is it?" I asked. It smelled of photocopier ink.

"My grandfather told me what the two of you had been talking about, and I had some extra time in the records room, so I did a little digging."

I looked up at him, and something in the redness to his cheeks and the way he wasn't quite looking at me told me some of that story was not strictly speaking true.

"Extra time in the records room, huh?" I said. But then I saw what I held in my hands. "Crime reports? From 1968?"

"Yeah," he said. "There were a bunch of case files for that address on that date, things that just got dropped without being solved."

"Like whatever happened to Coco's house," I said, flipping through the pages. There were a lot of pages.

"I don't know who Coco is," Nick said.

"She lived next door. In 1928."

"Oh."

My eyes were on the pages, not just because the details were interesting but because I could feel him processing so many things after I said "1928." I felt that little flinch first, where the idea of time travel dug at him, followed by a centering sort of breath, and then a deliberate attempt to... well, be cool with it.

"I checked out the article you already found first to match the details," he said. "Time and place, like that."

"Wow," I said, looking more closely.

"The article you had was just the beginning of a bunch of weird cases that got dropped," he said.

"What do you mean?" I asked.

"There were seven missing persons cases," he said.

"Seven?" I asked but then shook my head. Not my first question. "Why missing persons? Wouldn't it be assumed they died in the explosion?"

"No, look," he said, taking the folder back and reordering the pages. "There was an explosion on the morning of the Fourth of July. No one ever figured out what caused it aside from ruling out fireworks and the like, and the newspapers dropped the story without a single follow-up. Which is weird, but I think you'd have to find newspaper records to follow up on that."

I took a deep breath, choosing my words carefully. "There could have been magic involved," I said at last. "Some witches can make people forget things. Like they did with that wardrobe and everyone who saw it except you."

"Interesting," Nick said, looking back down at the papers. I could see a new flash of red to his cheeks, then that effort to be cool with it reasserted itself. "But then look here. This is the paperwork from the police who responded to the explosion. Three witnesses were interviewed. The weird thing is, they were three of the seven missing persons cases later. One of the other four cases was dropped; the woman was never missing in the first place I guess. Just a shut-in. But these three were never seen after these were taken."

Then he started handing me copies of old photographs. The first few were of the ruined building, better quality than the scanned newspaper.

Then I saw my mother, wrapped in a blanket and sitting in an ambulance. And then there was Marie Dubois and Lula Collins, standing together and talking to a bevy of men in uniform.

"They made witness statements?" I asked, seizing the folder back from him.

"Technically, yes? But they weren't very helpful," Nick said. "Just a lot of vagueness about hearing something outside and going out to investigate and not seeing anything."

"They all three gave witness statements?" I clarified as I shuffled through the papers.

"No, actually," Nick said, surprised. "The one in the ambulance photo didn't speak. She had a head injury, but the paramedics didn't think it was severe enough to have done brain damage. Either she was always mute, or she was just in shock. She had been so pregnant they were worried the trauma would induce labor."

"They didn't ever find out if she was mute or in shock?" I asked.

"No. They were all taken to a hospital to be checked over, but they disappeared while they were there and were never heard from again," he said.

I flipped through the last few pages, not really seeing the text my eyes were scanning over. "There were seven missing persons cases, you said?"

"Yes," he said. "These three, never solved. Three more who also had an association with this address. You know that plaque out front that says charm school? Apparently that was still a thing in 1968. From the looks of that plaque I always thought it was a lot longer ago than that, but I guess not."

"Patricia Dougherty, Debra St. John and Linda Sasse," I said, finding names on the appropriate forms.

"And Zenobia Weekes," Nick said, pointing to something deeper in the pile of papers. "She was reported missing but turned up here a month later, said she was never gone. I guess she didn't answer the door when the police knocked."

"She might have been busy," I said.

"Does this help? Whatever you're working on?" he asked.

"I think it does," I said and mustered up as much of a smile as I could manage. "Thanks."

"I can keep digging for more," he offered. "You might want to give me a few hints as to what you're looking for, though, so I don't tear off in the wrong direction."

It would be easier not to tell him. I hated how it felt like I was testing him every time I made any reference to magic.

But maybe that was why he had come. He wanted to test himself.

I flipped back through the folder and dug out the picture of my mother in the back of the ambulance.

"This is my mother," I said. "Kathleen Stinson. Sorry, Olgesen. I'm still getting used to all the names."

"Okay," he said cautiously, taking the photo from me to look at it more closely. "She does look like you." I could see it in his face, the question he was about to ask, but I pointed at the picture again, at the baby bump just barely visible under the folds of blanket.

"And that," I said, "is me."

I watched him absorb this and waited for that question to come bubbling back. He seemed to fight it, but in the end he had to ask. "Amanda, this picture is from 1968."

"Yes," I said. "And I was born in 1997. What happened in those few days which somehow jumped three decades is what we're working on now. That's our current mystery."

"Oh," he said. He looked from the photo in his hand to the one still in mine. "Oh, that one is Sophie's mother. And Brianna's there."

"Yes," I said.

"So it would help to dig up more on those names," he concluded.

I felt bad over how much I was taken by surprise that he wasn't just going to leave me with the folder and bow out of the rest of it.

"You can help? Really?" I said.

"Sure, no problem," he said. "I mean, I can't promise that I'll find anything."

"No, of course," I said, still feeling stunned.

"So I'll text you. Or should I call you? Maybe I should call if I find something big," he said.

"Whatever works for you," I said.

"You didn't block my number on your phone?" he asked.

"No! Why would I do that?" I asked. "Wait, were you trying to call me?"

"No," he admitted. "I'm sorry. That was a stupid question. You would never do that."

"Well, thanks for this," I said, holding up the folder. "Really. It means a lot."

"No problem," he said, putting his hat back on then retrieving his gloves from his pockets. "Look, if you ever get a hankering for someone to open up a bunch of cans, mix it all together in a dish and are it for about an hour, I know my grandfather would love to see you again. And Finnegan too."

"Oh," I said, looking from the folder in my hand to the ceiling, beyond which lay my waiting computer. "I might be tied up a lot in the next few days."

"Okay."

"Or weeks."

"I mean, obviously I meant me too. Not just Finnegan."

"I'm not trying to save your feelings," I said. I immediately wished I had found a better way to say that I wasn't looking to start maybe-dating again, as he flushed an even deeper crimson than before.

"Obviously."

"I mean, I'm not *just* trying to save your feelings," I said. "I'm not trying to avoid you without spelling it out. It's just, it might get dangerous here. I don't know. It might not be safe for you."

"But it's safe for you?"

I gripped the folder in my hands, the folder containing the missing persons reports for all three of our mothers. The unsolved missing persons cases.

I didn't need to say it out loud. Nick got it.

"Okay," he said, reaching for the door. "But if you ever need me, call me. I mean that."

I thought about explaining to him the sort of power that just might come gunning for me, but I decided not to. It wouldn't be kind to make him worry.

"I will," I promised.

I shut the door behind him and ran up the stairs.

"Look what I've got!" I called, brandishing the folder as I walked up to the table, but Sophie was clutching a stack of photos and papers of her own.

"No, look what we've got!" she said. She flashed me photograph after photograph. They weren't particularly good photographs, inexpertly taken with 1920s equipment, but they were good enough.

Good enough to show the faces of Patricia, Linda and Debra in 1928, not looking more than a day older than they had in that school photo.

CHAPTER 15

I sat with my legs curled up under a blanket, forehead resting on the cold pane of the window, looking out at the moonlight on the snow. It was my favorite place in the library, the place I went to when I was feeling most overwhelmed by everything I didn't know about magic, everything I still had to learn.

Usually it lent me a sense of comfort and bolstered my courage. But at the moment it just didn't feel right. It was my safe space, and yet it wasn't. Because while it was the right place, the particular one of the row of window seats in the library that was my preferred spot, it wasn't the right time.

And the wand I held in my hands felt even more wrong.

"This is completely useless, you know," I said, looking down at my wand.

"Organizing what we know is never useless," Brianna said from where she was taping photos to the library chalkboard. The same chalkboard that held our working timelines back in the present.

"No, I meant my wand," I said, tucking it away under my sweater.

"We might need to protect ourselves," Brianna said.

"If I need to protect myself, the very worst thing I could do would be to try to rely on that," I said.

Brianna hung the last of the photos then looked at me sorrowfully. "I'm sorry, Amanda. I'm afraid you're right. I don't know what's wrong with your wand, but I believe you when you tell me that it's still wrong."

"I should've left it at home," I said. "I still feel like it's spying on me."

"I thought that was just when you were trying to use it?" Sophie asked.

"Yes," I admitted. "The rest is just paranoia. Maybe. I don't like it touching me."

"We might be glad we brought it with later," Brianna said.

I didn't want to argue with that. It sounded dangerously close to Brianna letting an intuition guide her, and that was too weird to dwell on.

"What time was Otto going to get here?" I asked, looking out the window again.

"Eight," Sophie said, glancing at the clock. It was a quarter past eight. "I don't think we should start worrying just yet. He has a lot more going on than just our stuff."

"How busy can the gangster life be on a Sunday night?" I asked.

"So we have thirteen witches," Brianna said, redirecting our attention to the photos she had hung up on the board. Four columns, three rows, plus Evanora all on her own taped to the top frame of the board. "These three we know," Brianna said, writing the names under Patricia, Linda and Brenda. "And of course Evanora." She wrote that name as well. "What else do we know?"

"Not much," I grumbled.

"This one is just a kid," Sophie said. "Can't be more than ten. I don't want to imply all kids know each other, but maybe it would be worth checking with Coco?"

"Not if we don't have to," I said. "And daylight hours if we do."

"Agreed," Brianna said. Then she went back to the board and changed the position of some of the photos. "These two look like sisters, don't they?"

"Maybe," Sophie said. "Are we sure he didn't take pictures of the same woman twice? These two might be twins, or they might be the same woman."

"We can ask when he's here," Brianna said. "But thirteen. It's hard to argue with that total."

"Two more sisters," Sophie said.

"You think those are sisters?" Brianna asked.

"The hair is different colors, but look at their faces," Sophie said.

"Maybe," Brianna said in a slow drawl.

"So what's left?" Sophie asked, stepping back from the board. I pushed myself out of the window seat to come look.

"This woman, who looks older than time," Brianna said. "And this one, about twenty. And this one looks a little older, maybe Cynthia's age. Fifty or so."

"Aside from the three who were in the 60s with our mothers, are we assuming the rest are all of this time?" I asked.

"We would know if they were crossing our time portal," Brianna said.

"Unless they were here before we got here," I said. "Or had something like linked wardrobes, or access to another time portal."

"There are no other time portals in the US," Brianna said.

"Really?" Sophie asked.

"Yes, it's well-documented," she said. "There are two in Europe, in Russia and Germany specifically. There used to be one in Wales, but that stopped working in the early 1800s. There are two in Asia and three in Africa. Nothing in Australia, and so far as we know the same is true of Antarctica."

"What if someone created one?" I asked. "Could they keep it secret?"

"Miss Zenobia has a reputation for being exceedingly secretive," Brianna said. "Most witches gather in groups, like in Boston or the old world. But she struck out here alone, and she's never kept a witch student past the age of twenty or so. She sends them east if they want to continue learning."

"She was secretive because she was protecting the time portal?" I asked.

"That might have been her intent, but it failed," Brianna said. "Every witch I know of knows this time portal is here. The power needed to create something like that is so massive, even the least sensitive of witches feel like something just happened, even if they don't know what."

"So that's a no," I said.

We all heard the sound of a car pulling up to the curb out front and went down the stairs to open the door before anyone in the 1928 school could get there first. Otto came up the steps alone.

"No driver?" I asked, trying to see past the darkened windows of his car.

"Not tonight," he said. "I'm not letting Benny get mixed up in this."

"Good," I said and closed the door behind him. "Let's talk in the library. We're working on something."

But the moment we stepped back into the library Brianna gasped and rushed to the board.

"What is it?" Sophie asked.

"Someone's been writing on here," she said.

"Besides you?" Otto asked.

"Do you see anyone else here?" I asked, not sarcastically.

"Just you three," he said, sounding unsure if I was pulling his leg.

"Have you ever seen anyone else here besides us?" I asked.

"Sure," he said. "All the time. There's a whole gaggle of young ladies living here. Don't you chase them off when you're here? I assumed that's what you were doing."

"No," I said. "No, they're always here."

"Help me," Brianna said. "I have to take these photos back down."

"Why?" Sophie asked.

"Look," Brianna said, pointing to the board. Otto and I also drew closer to see.

Someone had taken the chalk to add some markings to the board. The woman we guessed to be Cynthia's age had a name now, Minnie Jackson, and a note that she was a former student. The woman in her early twenties was Alice Severson, and the note that said she was a current student had several exclamation points after it.

"Oh, crap," I said. "Current student? Like, she could be here now?"

"That's why we have to take this down," Brianna said.

"Look, there's another note," Sophie said, pointing to something under Evanora's photograph. It read, "not to be trusted."

"That much we already knew," I said.

Brianna copied everything from the board to the back of the photos then thrust them into her shoulder bag before erasing the board. Finally we turned our attention to Otto.

"These photos help a lot," Sophie said.

"Hopefully I can help even more," Otto said. "I've put a lot more street kids on the job trailing all of these women, and they've been mapping where they go."

He pulled a map out of his pocket and unfolded it, spreading it out on the library table. We weighted down the ends with books. Otto traced a fingertip over a mass of pencil tracings that reminded me too much of the scrawl of the brain fog spell.

"They are all over this part of town," he said. "But it's like a hurricane, this pattern. There's nothing going on in the center. And none of my street kids, not even the craftiest, have seen where they're actually coming from. They just step around a corner and disappear, every time."

"There are spells for that," Sophie said. "Tell the kids it's not their fault, and that we appreciate their efforts. This is perfect."

"How does it help?" Otto asked. "There are several blocks in the center of this pattern. That's a lot of ground to search."

"But search it we must," Brianna said. "Neither you nor your street kids are going to be able to find their hiding place. It could be as tall as a skyscraper, and you'd never see it."

"It's invisible?" Otto asked.

"Not so much invisible as just really hard to notice," Brianna said. "You might see it, but your eyes would keep moving past it, and you'd forget in a fraction of a second it was even there."

"A spell like that could disguise an entire building?" I asked.

"Of course," Brianna said, blinking at me in surprise. "There was

111

one over the school until Sophie and I took it down. Don't you remember?"

I did remember, now that she was mentioning it. I had had the devil's time finding the place when I'd first arrived. Even the GPS on my phone had seemed confused.

"But we can find it," Sophie said to Otto. "Can you give us a lift?"

"Not just yet," Otto said, folding up the map and stuffing it back in his pocket. "I want to recon one more time first. I'll find a place where I'm sure it's safe inside the eye of that storm, and then I'll take you there."

"You'll be in more danger than we'd ever be," I said. "We have protections that hide us from those witches, not to mention power of our own."

"I'm not helpless," Otto said, patting what I assumed was the outline of a gun under his coat.

"I have an idea," Brianna said. "But I need more time here in the library to try it out."

"Maybe-" I started to say, but Sophie cut me off.

"The three of us absolutely are not splitting up," she said. "Absolutely not."

"If those witches were looking to hurt me, they've had ample opportunity to try," Otto said. "They watch me, but they've never tried to stop me."

"They know you're here now," I said. "They know what that might mean."

"I'll be fine," he said. "I just want to set up a few basic defenses then I'll be right back here to move you in."

"I need the time," Brianna reminded me.

"Fine," I agreed, throwing up my hands. "But call off your street kids. All of them. I don't want kids getting hurt."

"I will," Otto promised.

I watched from the window seat as his car pulled away from the curb, heading back towards the riverfront. I expanded my awareness wider and wider, but if anyone besides me were watching him in that moment, I didn't sense it.

I wished that made me feel better.

CHAPTER 16

*W*e didn't really know all the rules about how the magic worked that divided us from the students who were all around us in the charm school in 1928. At first I thought we had to leave the room to make things appear in 1928 like the letter for Otto or the photographs on the chalkboard.

But Brianna decided to test whether just not touching a thing, not looking at it, was enough. So she found a pad of paper in one of the library drawers and wrote out a question, leaving it next to her on the table as she sorted through the photographs and consulted her notebook.

"What are you asking them?" I asked.

"For more information on Minnie, Alice, and Evanora," Brianna said, handing some of the photographs to me and the other half to Sophie.

"What sort of information? A home address or something?" Sophie asked.

"No, what their powers are," Brianna said. "I want to know their specialties."

"What if the student talking to you isn't a witch?" I asked.

"They are noticing things appearing and disappearing and are helping us out rather than panicking," Sophie pointed out. "They're witches."

"Okay," I agreed.

"I've cataloged all of the spells used to hide the main one that was triggered by Miss Zenobia's box," Brianna said. "Some I know for sure. I mean, obviously one of them can affect memory, and another simply has to have some form of time magic."

"Time magic," I said, fighting a wave of panic. "I thought you said it was rare?"

"It is," Brianna said. "But one of these thirteen must have some ability. Too many of the spells had that element to them. Didn't you see?"

I closed my eyes and cast my mind back. "I did," I admitted. "Some of the spells were elegant, like braids made from the threads I can see. Most were scribbles, though."

"How complex were the braids?" Sophie asked.

"I don't know," I said. "I don't have enough to compare it to."

"One of them has time magic," Brianna said again, "but not a lot of control, or not a lot of power, or both. Otherwise, they would have taken the time bridge from us by now."

"Or tried to," I said, curling a hand into a fist.

"It may yet come to that," Brianna said. "We need to figure out what it is they don't want us to know."

"So we have no clue which of them is a time witch," Sophie said, shuffling through her half of the photographs. "I don't think we'll know anything by looking at them. Not about their powers."

"Look," I said, pointing to Brianna's notepad. New writing, not her own spiky cursive but a more elegant script, was now covering the bottom part of the page.

"This feels like passing notes in class," Sophie said.

"Okay, the girl who is writing to me says her name is May," Brianna said. "She's a witch but is too young to train with Alice. She only knows that Alice borrows spells from others to work into talismans and amulets."

"Borrows?" I said.

"Eh, the girl might not grasp the concepts entirely," Brianna said. "Let's assume she can't do the spell herself, but she can fix it to things."

"Like, say, everything inside the walls of this house?" I said.

"Exactly," Brianna said, then continued reading down the page. "Minnie was a student here decades ago, but she used to come back to teach things to the younger girls. Apparently she can summon and control electricity."

"Wow," I said. "That's quite a power."

"Did we see anything like that in the spells we dismantled?" Sophie asked.

Brianna flipped through her notebook. "Not precisely," she said as she scanned pages. "But there were a few that involved certain... attractions? I can follow what she was doing, but I'm not sure how much you two know about electromagnetism. It's hard to explain if you don't get that."

"Can you try a metaphor?" Sophie asked.

"Well," Brianna said, then sat up straighter as a thought hit her. "You know in movies or TV shows about science nerds, how they sometimes do these really elaborate pranks? It's not science, no one would think it was, but if you got pranked if one of these elaborate tricks, you'd know it was the physics majors from the science hall, right?"

"Because the elaborate pranks would require physics knowledge to pull off," Sophie said.

"Exactly. It's like that, only with spells. None of the spells were actually electrical, but she's using her knowledge of how electricity works to make these other spells."

"Like pranks?" I asked, still confused.

"No, her work was mainly joining together some of the other spells," Brianna said. "Opposites attract, right? She could fuse spells of opposite effects together so smoothly I nearly couldn't tease them apart to dismantle them."

"How long do you think they were planning this?" I asked. "Months and months, or on the fly?"

"That I would really love to know," Brianna said, looking back at her notepad. "May doesn't know much about Evanora, except the students have sometimes seen her about town and Miss Zenobia has warned them all never to speak to her and to run from her if necessary."

"So past Miss Zenobia knows this is a problem but isn't solving it?" I said.

"Miss Zenobia's job is to protect the time portal in the orchard, not to rid the world of troublesome witches," Brianna said. "And I wouldn't rule out her knowing we're here and leaving it to us to take care of Evanora." She tore off the sheet and stuffed it in her bag then wrote another question on the fresh page.

"What are you asking now?" Sophie asked.

"If they've seen any of them around, and when," Brianna said. "We know they've been letting Otto see them. I imagine they're keeping themselves well away from Miss Zenobia. But they might be lingering around, watching the school to see when Miss Zenobia is occupied. Might be worth knowing."

"No time," Sophie said, getting up from the table as we all heard the distinctive hum of the motor of Otto's car. "Best not leave that out. Let's go."

"I wish we had narrowed it down more," Brianna said, stuffing her things back into her bag and double-checking she had her wand inside her coat. I touched my own, fighting the urge to flinch at the feel of its shape through the wool. "From what you described, Evanora sounds like she has glamour magic, illusions and that."

"She also had memory magic, right?" I said. "She made everyone but Nick forget about the wardrobe and the body that she took from the police station."

"That might not have been her even if that note she left implied it," Brianna said. "It's highly unlikely she has so much skill in two different disciplines."

We let the matter drop, running down the stairs to reach the door before Otto could knock. He smiled his usual flirty smile at Sophie, gave Brianna a quick nod of hello, and then looked at me for the briefest of moments before looking away.

Something was wrong.

"Otto," I said, stepping closer to catch at the sleeve of his coat.

"It will be fine," he said. "I'll keep him safe; you have my word."

"Keep who safe?" Sophie asked. "You said you'd keep Benny out of it."

"And so I have," Otto said, spinning the ring of keys in his hand as if demonstrating that he was the driver this evening.

"No," I said. "Otto, no way."

"Who is it?" Sophie demanded, exasperated.

But Brianna had already connected the dots. "It's Edward. He's in the car."

"He saw me leave here earlier and found me at the club," Otto said, putting his hand on mine still gripping his coat and using it to guide me down the front walk to the car. "He knows something is up. There's no getting rid of him now. And really, he's probably safer with you than anywhere else."

"That's likely true," Brianna said.

"He's worried about you," Otto said. "He's been watching this place constantly since New Year's Eve. He's missed so much work his job is in jeopardy. And nothing I can say is putting him at ease. He needs to hear it from you."

"I can't put him at ease either," I said, but Otto just opened the back door and all but shoved me into the seat next to Edward. Brianna squeezed in after me, Sophie taking the front seat next to Otto.

"Hi," Edward said, adjusting his hat as if he had considered taking it off to greet me then thought better of it.

"I wanted to keep you out of this," I said. "I worked very hard to keep you out of this."

"Well, I'm in it," Edward said. Otto pulled out into the sparse traffic with a lurch that threw me against Edward. I might have been a touch too forceful in getting myself back into the middle of the seat.

"Hey," Edward said gently.

"Sorry," I grumbled.

"Amanda, I'm not here to make you uncomfortable or make any awkward speeches," he said. "You made your feelings very clear, and I respect that. But after what I saw at Mina Fox's house and what happened on New Year's Eve, I know that whenever I see you, trouble is coming close behind you, and you can use some allies."

"I would prefer not to put you into danger," I said.

"But Otto you're willing to thrust into any fire?" he asked.

Otto barked out a laugh that stopped when Sophie poked him hard in the ribs.

"Otto is different," I said.

"How?" Edward asked. "We grew up the same. We developed the same skills to get by. I can hold my own, same as him."

I didn't ask him to elaborate. I felt the gun he wore on his hip every time the jostling of the car threw me against him.

"You chose a different path, buddy," Otto said.

"And we all know how that worked out," Edward said. "Maybe the other path should've been mine all along."

"Not if I have anything to say about it," Otto said.

"Apparently you don't, since he's here now," I said.

"He's here now, and there's no getting rid of him," Otto said. "In fact, we're all here. If you witches wouldn't mind doing whatever it is you do. I want to hide the car, and it won't do any good if your friends know just where I do it."

I closed my eyes, expanding my awareness, all too aware that I'd not yet sensed any of them when they didn't want me to.

"I think it's clear," I said at last.

"Me too," Sophie agreed.

Otto checked all of his mirrors. The nearest cars were a block behind us, even farther away in front. He switched off his lights then made a sharp left turn in the middle of the block. I nearly screamed, certain he was driving us all into a brick wall even as he gunned the accelerator. But there was an alley. It was almost too narrow for the car, and he lost the mirror on his passenger side to something protruding from the bricks.

Then we were in a sort of courtyard between the buildings. The space was still tight, but we could just ease the doors open enough to squeeze out of the car and follow Otto to a stack of garbage cans.

"Where are we?" I asked, whispering although I wasn't sure why.

"Center of the hurricane," Otto said, and he and Edward started pulling cans aside until a doorway was exposed. Otto opened it with a swift kick and waved us all inside.

Without a word between them, Sophie and Brianna both pulled their wands and cast spells to fill the space within with magical light. The silvery glow was too bright at first, but it settled down to a level just strong enough to illuminate what appeared to be an abandoned warehouse. The rafters hung with dust-clogged spiderwebs, and the tiles were stained with streaks of leaks past, but the only crates or barrels I saw now were a pile of damaged ones in the far corner.

"What's the plan?" Edward asked as Sophic and Brianna circled the interior of the building.

"I don't know if we have one yet," I admitted. Then Sophie and Brianna came back to stand with us nearer the door, wands lowered. "Anything?"

"No other doors than this one, which was blocked by those cans," Sophie said.

"I think it's just what it looks like," Brianna said. "A building that time forgot. It certainly doesn't smell like anyone's been in here in years."

"No, squatters leave a distinctive odor," Otto said. "You'd know if anyone had been in here."

"How did you find it?" I asked.

"Careful inspection of a lot of maps," he said. "This is going to work perfectly."

"For what?" I asked.

"For a trap," he said. "You three can set up here, whatever it is you do."

"There are wards," Brianna said, still looking around. "Protective spells. Defensive ones." Then she looked at Otto, giving him a wide grin. "Magic circles can be very effective for traps."

"And what are we doing in the meantime?" Edward asked.

"That's easy, my friend," Otto said, slipping an arm around Edward's shoulders. "You and me, we're bait."

CHAPTER 17

*A*ll of those mornings with all of those rituals to maintain the integrity of the time bridge had given the three of us an acute awareness of each other's magic. It was paying off now, when time was short and we didn't want the vulnerability of putting ourselves into a deep state removed from the world around us.

Not that I was much use. I could pull energy from the world around us, but without my wand I couldn't direct it towards any goal. I could just pass it to Sophie and Brianna as they worked. But I knew that was important too. Whatever happened next, we would be in real trouble if any of us were exhausted before the fight even began.

Sophie danced around the perimeter of the space, the toes of her shoes leaving loopy sweeps in the dust of ages that was piled up thicker nearer the walls. I kept my awareness in the physical world, but I still sensed what she was doing. It was like I could feel the hairs on the back of my neck lifting up, particularly when her dance spiraled closer to me. She was cloaking us and protecting us and leaving ribbons of energy that would function like laser lights in a museum vault. She would know if anything crossed them, even if the warehouse were to be plunged back into darkness.

Brianna in the meantime was focusing on conjuring a magic circle.

This was different than the one we had done before when we'd removed the fog from our brains. This time she was standing outside of the space she had defined on the floor with another long crocheted chain of yarn. I watched the tip of her wand as she swished it over and over again, drawing arcane shapes in the air to match the words she was constantly chanting. She worked her way around the circle several times, always adding more and more layers to her spells.

I didn't like Otto and Edward being our bait, not even when Otto amended his plan from both of them being bait to Otto being bait and Edward being backup.

But I also couldn't argue that his plan was probably the best we were going to come up with. If any of the three of us went out looking for witches, we'd surely find ourselves dealing with all thirteen, not a single one alone. None of them would risk it.

But Otto on his own? He could lure one in. A single witch wouldn't fear for her safety, especially if she only intended to follow him, to see where he went. She probably wouldn't even be bothered if she noticed Edward trailing them.

A single witch, trapped inside our magic circle. Surely we had enough power together, the three of us, to hold just one. To get some answers.

So Sophie had wrapped Otto in a magical breeze that followed him like an irresistible aroma, sure to catch the attention of anyone sensitive to magic. She tried to make it look like he'd just passed too close to some innocent spell she had been spinning, but we had no idea if that ruse would work.

But maybe it didn't matter. They were watching Otto to get to us. If they didn't take the bait, though, I wasn't sure what we'd do next.

They were waiting for something, but what?

"He's coming," Sophie said, stopping her dance in mid-spin.

"To the shadows," Brianna said and extinguished the lights with a flick of her wand. She and Sophie disappeared towards the back of the building, but I moved over to the pile of broken barrels and crates, to be closer to the door. I crouched low, one hand on the cold tile of the warehouse floor.

My other hand inched toward my wand, but I felt a spasm like I'd bumped my funny bone. The wand was still not my friend. I touched Cynthia's amulet instead. At least it was still protecting me.

There was a loud bang as Otto once more opened the door with a swift kick. Then he strolled into the darkness of the warehouse, hands in pockets and feet shuffling through the dust, whistling as if this was all entirely normal for close to midnight on a Sunday night.

I saw a shadow in the doorway, an inky shape scarcely outlined against the darkness of the courtyard beyond. I could see no details, just a general sense of a human-shaped figure wearing a voluminous hood. One of the witches.

Then I felt that strange spasm again tingling up my arm, and I could swear that my wand was trying to jump out of the hidden pocket inside my coat. I slapped my hand on it, but to the touch it was as inert as ever.

Otto was still whistling and trying to feign like he was looking for something, but since the room was empty it wasn't very convincing.

The figure in the doorway advanced silently into the room, seeming to bring that deeper darkness with her through the gloom. She was drawing closer to the spot where Brianna had cast her magic circle, but her progress was painfully slow across the floor.

Then someone else was in the doorway, almost as silent as that ghostly figure. Edward. He slipped inside the warehouse then gently eased the door shut. Then he reached for a metal pole left leaning against the wall near the door and fit one end at about the point where a doorknob should be then wedged the other end in the tiled floor.

There was a soft hiss and then a click as the pipe locked into place. Softer than a mouse's sneeze, and yet the shadowy figure in the middle of the room stopped and turned back.

She wasn't in the circle. Not yet.

I could feel Brianna and Sophie near me. I didn't even have to go into the world of threads to sense them now. They were waiting the same as I was. Just a few more steps. Their anxiety was like a scream inside my head. I had to tune it out.

125

Otto had reached the far wall of the warehouse. He lit a match, holding it high as if to examine the bricked-over doorway before him.

Still, the shadow didn't move those last few steps. Otto knew she hadn't, because if she had the three of us would've come out of hiding. But she had stopped following him. He had run out of options.

He turned just as the match burned down. I got a brief glimpse of his face before the light sputtered out. I could hear him digging another out of the box, but I also saw something else.

The shadow was moving. Not forward, not like we wanted her to. No, she was planting her feet as if preparing to make an attack.

She was drawing her wand.

There was a scraping sound as Otto struck the match, but by then I was already halfway across the warehouse, arms out in front of me as I charged at the shadow.

My feet might have been too loud, slapping on the tile as I ran. But then, I was pretty sure I was also yelling some sort of battle cry. At any rate, the woman heard me coming and lowered the wand she had aimed at Otto, turning back to see me instead.

It was Evanora. Her eyes widened as she saw me barreling down on her, but she had no time to raise her wand. I struck her square in the middle, lifting her off of the floor and hurling her into Brianna's circle.

She shrieked, and there was a flash of light as the spells triggered, but I didn't get a good look at it because my own feet were slipping over the dusty tiles. I was going to tumble into the magic circle myself.

Not a scenario we had prepped for. But there was nothing to catch myself with but the floor.

Then my coat hiked up, choking me as I was propelled back. Away from the circle. Into Edward's arms.

"Steady," he said, holding me until I got my feet under me, his eyes never leaving the light show in the middle of the room.

Evanora was not pleased. She was screaming in anger, but the words she was screaming were spells. She directed them with her wand, but each fizzled and died on impact with Brianna's circle. The light at each impact was blinding, and the air was filling with the smell of ozone. My hair was standing straight on end like the bride of Frankenstein.

But we were safe.

Brianna and Sophie came out of the shadows, circling around to join Edward and I. Then Otto too was with us. We all watched as Evanora finally expended the last of her power in a useless display that made not so much as a crack in Brianna's spells.

"Finished?" I asked. Evanora just seethed. Her hood had fallen back, the cloak hanging crookedly from her shoulders. She must have pushed her power too hard, to judge from the thin trickle of blood running down from one nostril.

I thought she was going to renew her attacks on the circle, with her fists if that was all she had left, but then she seemed to pull herself together. She took out a handkerchief and pressed it to her nose, then smoothed down her hair and straightened her clothing until she was once more the dazzling moll that could banter with gangsters like an equal.

"Your plan isn't going to work," she said to us. Then her eyes darted over to Otto. "Mr. Meyer. You're going to be in so much hot water."

Otto just shrugged.

"We're going to ask you some questions," Brianna said, taking out her notebook.

"Spare me," Evanora said, rolling her eyes. "I have nothing to say to the likes of you."

"We're curious about your magic," Brianna said.

"That's what you're starting with? My magic? You're not even going to ask me who I work for? But that's my favorite bit." She drew herself into a stance meant to evoke a mobster's heavy and lowered her voice to a hoarse growl. "Who do you work for?"

"Despite the note you left in our time, I don't think you're the one with time magic," Brianna went on as if Evanora hadn't said anything at all. She glanced up from her notebook and gave Brianna a hard look, like a stern teacher waiting for an answer. Then she looked back down at her book. "No? Didn't think so. I doubt you're the one affecting anyone's memories either. Again, despite your little note."

"I can make men remember me," Evanora said, letting her cloak slip from her shoulders and giving Otto a smoldering look. Brianna looked at Otto like a scientist checking for observable effects from an experiment, but Otto just shrugged.

"That's a no," Brianna said and ticked something off in her book. Then she looked up at Evanora again and tipped her head to one side assessingly. "You know, I don't think you're even the one summoning up the glamours."

"Oh, I'm glamorous enough," Evanora said. She tried to direct her attentions at Edward this time, but I planted my feet further apart and put my hands on my hips, blocking him from her view.

She smirked at me, not intimidated.

"No, even that is a very disciplined branch of magic, and you don't strike me as particularly disciplined," Brianna said.

"She's a troublemaker," Sophie said, and Brianna's eyes suddenly widened.

"What is it?" I asked. Brianna had been throwing a bit of acting into her questions before, but this sudden realization response struck me as genuine.

"Give me your wand," she said, holding out her hand.

"What? Why?"

"Because I know what's wrong with it now," she said. I pulled out the wand, glad for the gloves I still wore, and laid it on Brianna's bare palms.

Brianna held it up, rolling it between her fingertips as she shot Evanora a triumphant look. Evanora said nothing, but there was a new wariness to her eyes.

"I know what your magic is," Brianna said, shifting the wand to hold it vertically in one hand by the very tips of her fingers. "You have a tainting magic, don't you? You darken things. Ruin them. Spoil milk, sicken cattle, destroy crops. You're that kind of witch. Aren't you?"

Evanora's eyes narrowed, but still she said nothing.

"Yes, I see it now," Brianna said, looking closely at my wand. "And I see just how to peel it away."

She ran her hand up the length of my wand, and I felt that motion like a wave traveling through my body.

It wasn't pleasant. It was like someone was pulling at all of the threads that formed me all at once. And some of them were snapping.

I startled to fall to my knees, but Edward was still supporting me. His arms tightened, lending me some strength.

I looked up at Brianna, who was watching me with concern. She hadn't meant to hurt me. But now my wand was glowing so brightly in her hand. Cleansed. Renewed. My ally once more.

And in her other hand was a mass of black ooze. I don't know exactly what the smell was that was coming off of it. Rot, but like no rot smell I had ever been assaulted with. It made me long for the freshness of that ozone smell.

Brianna grinned and tossed me my wand. I caught it. It felt so right in my hand. I swung it around, throwing sparks everywhere. Happy sparks. I laughed aloud and gestured up to the center of the peaked ceiling, creating a miniature shower of fireworks that rained down all around Evanora, hissing when they struck the circle around her.

"Mine is a small power," Evanora said sullenly. "But I'm not the one you should be afraid of. And you should be afraid. Very afraid. You shouldn't be playing games, you little pretend witches."

"We're not playing games," Sophie said.

"This is a game. This is all a game," Evanora said then bubbled over with evil laughter.

"You're awfully cocky for someone in a trap she can't get out of," Otto said.

Evanora laughed even harder at that. "I'm exactly where I'm meant to be," she said. "Right here. Right now. Where my employer wants me to be. Where I'll be until my employer says otherwise."

"She's bluffing," Sophie said, but she didn't sound sure.

"Very well," Brianna said to Evanora. "Who do you work for?"

Evanora licked her lips, as if she found that question absolutely delicious. Then she grinned at us. "I'll never tell."

"Fine. Have it your way," Brianna said and flung the black ooze at the circle. She made a small motion with her wand with her other hand, opening an aperture in the magic circle just large enough and just long enough to let the ooze inside. "Have your spell back," Brianna said.

The ooze hit Evanora square in the face, which might have been funny until she started screaming.

CHAPTER 18

*B*ack home in Iowa, I had lived in an apartment, but that apartment had been on the edge of a pretty small town. Our windows had overlooked the beginnings of farmland, some corn fields but more dairy farms. Lots of cows and a few other farm animals, but also coyotes. I only rarely caught a glimpse of one, but at night I could hear them calling to each other.

And I could hear them celebrating a successful hunt. The sound of their cries had woken me on many a summer night, and some winter ones as well.

But worse than their triumphant howling had been the dying sounds of their prey. I know it's not technically murder. They weren't human. They were hunting for food they needed to live.

But the sounds of those animals shrieking through a painful death haunt me still.

Evanora, clawing at the ooze that appeared to be soaking into her face, sounded like one of those animals. It was horrific.

"Help her," Sophie said.

"I don't know what's happening," Brianna said, blinking back tears. "This shouldn't be happening. It's her own spell."

"Can't you make it stop?" Sophie asked.

"I'll drop the circle," Brianna said, but Otto caught her wrist before she could raise her wand.

"No," he said. "It's a trick."

"It can't be," Sophie said. "She can't be acting. No one is that good."

"We can't risk it," Otto said. "Do not let her out or all of our lives are forfeit."

"He's right," I said, forcing the words past the lump in my throat. "Look, that ooze is almost gone."

"Because it's inside her," Sophie said.

But as the last of the black ooze slipped into the corners of her eyes, Evanora's screams finally quieted. She was on her knees now, slumped over so that her hair covered her face. I could see her shoulders moving as she heaved in breath after breath. Breaths that were hitching with pain. But at least she was quiet.

"She's not going to tell us anything," Otto said. "And the longer we're here, the more likely the others will find us. Are you ready for that fight?"

"No," Brianna said, still looking sickened from what she had just done to Evanora.

"So what do we do now?" Edward asked. "If we don't let her go, what other options are there?"

"We can't move her," Brianna said. "The spells are bound to place. I could come up with spells that would hold with the car, but that would take time."

"Where would we even move her to?" Sophie asked. "We can't bring her to the school. We can't dump her on the students there now."

"Maybe we just leave her here," Brianna said. "She can't get herself out."

"The rest of her coven could free her," I said.

"It would take time. It would buy us some time," Brianna said.

"No," Otto said. "She's a threat. We have to end that threat."

"The coven is the threat," Sophie said.

"Which we'll end one witch at a time," Otto said. He drew his gun, but this time, it was Sophie grabbing his wrist and keeping him from raising his arm.

From inside the magic circle, Evanora started to make some sort of choking noise. It took me a moment to figure out she was laughing at us. Then she sat back, tossing the hair out of her eyes to fix her gaze on Otto.

"I'm not afraid of you," she said to him. "I'm not afraid of death. But you should be."

"Sophie, let me go," he said.

"No. It's too bloody. It'll lead back to you. You don't need that kind of trouble," she said.

"No one will ever find her body," he said.

"Sophie is right," I said.

"Then you do it," he said, pulling his wrist out of Sophie's grasp and putting his gun away. "You can do it and never leave a trace. I know you can."

"No, Otto," I said. He stepped closer to me to whisper close to my ear.

"I'll take Edward out of here first, if that helps," Otto said.

"I'm not leaving," Edward, who was still standing close behind me, said.

"I can deal with her," I said. "But I'm not going to kill her. What I did before, I'm not doing that again."

"What did you do before?" Edward asked, but none of us answered him.

"What are you thinking, Amanda?" Sophie asked.

"I can bind her," I said. "I can remove her from the flow of time. I've seen how it can be done. I understand it. I can do it."

Evanora, sitting on her heels, was watching me with great interest. I waited for her to say something, to perhaps tell me that she didn't fear me any more than she feared Otto's gun, but she held her peace. She was just watching me.

Everyone was watching me.

Then Sophie and Brianna traded a long look.

"Do you mean like Juno bound to the time bridge?" Brianna asked. "Or like Mina Fox bound to the crystal ball?"

"Either," I said. I looked down at my hands, flexing my fingers. "I've seen the way to manipulate the threads. I know I can do it."

"You've seen it because it was shown to you," Sophie said. "But we don't know by who or for what purpose. For all we know, it could've been her mysterious employer."

"It wasn't shown to me," I said. "I figured it out myself."

"When you were flooded with power," Sophie said.

"This is my power," I said. "I'm not under anyone's influence. I know I can do this. Everyone will be safer if I do this."

"But can you undo it?" Brianna asked. "If you trap her outside of time, can you free her again? Because we can't get Mina back out of that crystal ball. And Juno is so deeply a part of that time bridge we can't even perceive her unless she chooses to reveal herself to us."

"I think so," I said. "I'll be able to figure it out if I keep working the problem. But why would we ever want to?"

"Because if you remove her from time and we can't ever bring her back, that sounds like a fate worse than death," Brianna said. "Is that what we do?"

"If we let her go, or if we leave her here until her coven frees her, we put everyone here in danger," I said. "Otto and his entire organization, Edward, the students at the school, maybe even Coco and her family."

"We'll find a way to protect them," Brianna said.

"How?" I asked.

"I don't know, but we'll figure something out. It's what we do," Brianna said.

"We figure out what our mothers knew," Sophie said. "The thing they don't want us to know. The thing that's probably the key to how to defeat them."

Evanora was snickering again.

"Do you have anything to say?" Brianna demanded, pointing her wand at Evanora, who just kept laughing.

"I don't like this," Otto said. "It feels like a trap. She's stalling us."

CHARM HIS PANTS OFF

"The others can't get near without us knowing," Sophie said. "We warded the whole building. This was our trap, remember?"

"And I was the bait," Otto said. "Only now it feels like maybe she was the bait. She followed me knowing it was a trap, and now she's holding us here."

"Are you bait?" Brianna asked Evanora.

"You three aren't as clever as you think you are," Evanora said.

"That's not an answer," Sophie said. "Are you holding us here? Are you stalling?"

"It's not my fault if you three don't have a plan," Evanora scoffed. "I suppose you could make me answer every one of your questions, but you'd have to torture me to get me to talk. And you don't have the backbone for that."

Now I was the one brandishing my wand as I stepped up to the very edge of the magic circle. "Who do you work for?" I demanded. Edward tugged at the back of my coat, trying to pull me away from the circle, but I brushed him off without taking my eyes off Evanora.

"Are you going to make me talk?" she asked me, almost purring as she spoke.

"I don't think I have to," I said. "I think I can just read the answers in your threads."

"Try it," she said. "Go ahead. Read my whole life story. I'll wait."

I was vaguely aware of a whispered conversation behind me, of Otto trying to convince Edward to go wait in the car. Otto seemed to think I was about to unleash my darkest powers. But I wasn't. I didn't have to hurt Evanora to get the answers. I just had to look.

"Amanda!" Sophie cried out just as my eyes were about to close. "Don't do it!" She edged herself between me and the magic circle, forcing me to take half a step back.

"No, this is the best way," I said. "I'm not going to pull her out of time or hurt her at all. I'm just going to see what's really going on here."

"Don't," Sophie said. "Look at her. Look how badly she wants this."

I looked past Sophie to Evanora still kneeling on the floor. Her eyes were shining brightly with more anticipation than a roomful of kids on Christmas morning.

"She wants you to do this," Brianna said. "She wants it very badly."

"But why?" I asked. "What would she gain? It makes no sense."

"Just do it," Evanora said to me, still looking like the cat who ate the canary. "Just blink yourself to that other world and take a look around."

"*That's* the trap," Otto said. "It's not for all of you. It's just for Amanda."

I wanted to object again. It still made no sense to me at all. But before I could put any words together, I saw Evanora throw up her hands.

"I give up," she said to the room at large. "I did give it my best shot."

"Gave what your best shot?" I asked. But she just got back to her feet and made a big show of brushing the dust from the floor off of her cloak and dress.

"My way would've been easier," she said. "But whatever."

And then the warehouse around us started melting.

CHAPTER 19

*W*e weren't inside an abandoned warehouse. We had never been inside an abandoned warehouse.

I watched in horror as the illusion of dusty tiles dried up like puddles on the floor, revealing a gleaming marble floor of white with veins of gold. At first, I thought it was glowing, throwing up light that burned away the cobwebbed shadows, but as the shabby brick walls became gleaming marble columns and panels of wood the color of golden honey, I realized that light was merely a reflection.

I looked up. And up. And up. The warehouse had been all one space but as tall as a two-story building. Whatever we were in now just kept going, level after level, balcony after balcony. Every level had more columns, the columns adorned with art deco light fixtures that all added up to an almost overwhelming brightness.

I couldn't count how many floors there were between where we were standing and the glass ceiling above us offering glimpses of the night sky, but it was a lot. We had to be standing in the tallest building in St. Paul. It had to be taller than anything in Minneapolis in 1928 too. I wouldn't have been surprised if it was taller than anything in either city in 2019.

It simply couldn't be real.

And yet, as much as my brain was insisting that the warehouse was real and this was the illusion, my gut didn't believe it.

"What is this place?" Otto whispered.

"This is home," Evanora said.

And then she stepped out of Brianna's magic circle as if it also had never really existed. Brianna gasped.

"Get back," I said to the others as Evanora stepped up towards me. "Get back!"

Sophie caught Brianna's arm and pulled her back towards where the door used to be, but judging from Otto's swearing, it wasn't there anymore.

"We meet again, little witch," Evanora said to me with a smile. I raised my wand, but her smile never wavered. There was the sound of a scuffle from behind me. Otto was wrestling with Edward.

"Keep him safe for me, Otto," I said without turning.

"There is no safety for any of you here," Evanora said. "You just waltzed straight into the center of our web. You wrapped yourselves up and presented yourselves as so much spider food."

"Come on," I said. "We both know I didn't do what you wanted."

"You haven't yet," Evanora said with a shrug. "But you will."

"No. You can't make me," I said.

"Evanora has her talents," someone else said, her voice echoing throughout the tower's interior, bouncing up to the top then back down to the bottom so that it sounded like this one woman was surrounding all of us. I searched the space around me, trying to look behind every column and decorative plant, around the benches and over-stuffed chairs. "She is not the least of us," the voice went on as I took another step back from Evanora, trying to look everywhere at once, "but she is far from the best."

Evanora stepped back with a little bow, and finally I saw the other woman. She was walking towards me, flanked by two other women. They were all wearing cocktail dresses in pastel colors. The clothes and the confident way they were walking, they looked like they'd just stepped out of a late 60s spy film.

But they were young. The elegance of their clothing made them seem older at first glance, but when I looked more closely, none of them could be much more than eighteen. And yet that voice had carried a power not to be taken lightly.

"You're Patricia Dougherty," I said to the one in the middle. She still wore her long blonde hair straight and loose. Except for the clothes, she looked exactly like the photograph from the school.

"And you're Amanda... well, I guess you call yourself Clarke," she said with a sneering smile. "You look just like your mother."

"Don't use my mother to taunt me," I said, still holding my wand raised although I had no idea what I could do with it that would be of any use.

"I would never," Patricia said, putting a hand over her heart. "Your mother and I were dear friends."

"That's not the picture I've been getting," I said. "You tried to make us forget our mothers. Why?"

"But you didn't forget, did you?" Patricia said.

"We did. If not for random chance, we'd not remember them now," I said.

"Random chance. That always comes up at some point, doesn't it? One can almost count on it," Patricia said.

"What are you saying?" I asked.

"I'm saying the point of our spell wasn't to make you forget so much as to make sure you took a really close look at what you remembered," Patricia said. "What you remembered, and what you didn't. Because you were never told."

I looked back at Brianna and Sophie to see what they thought of this. They came closer to stand beside me.

"Why all the spells if that was all you wanted?" Brianna asked. "Why didn't you just stop by the school and leave us a message?"

"I confess, it was a test," Patricia said. "You passed, by the way."

"Full marks," said Linda.

"Nice work," said Debra.

"I particularly liked how you worked out getting the current class of students to help you," Linda said. "That was very clever."

Brianna bit her lip but said nothing. I was sure she had the same question as I did. How did they know about that? It had happened just hours ago.

"So this has all been a test?" I asked. "Following Otto around for months was a test? Everything that happened on New Year's Eve? That was also a test? People died."

"Charlotte was always going to do what she was going to do," Patricia said. "We were just there to watch you."

"You gave her an amulet to cloak her from our perceptions," I said. Patricia just shrugged, which really made me angry. "Without your help she never would've been able to kill Thomas."

"Of course she would have," Patricia said. "She did. You can't change history, you know."

"You put a skyscraper right on the riverfront in 1928 St. Paul," I said. "That's historical?"

"No one will ever find it, so it's not ahistorical," Patricia said.

"This isn't right," Brianna said. "There are rules."

"Rules? Really?" Patricia all but snapped. "We didn't ask to be here. We didn't ask to be stuck here. And yet here we are, because of your mothers. So sue us for trying to make it just a touch more livable until we can get home."

"Back to 1968?" I asked. "That's not how the time portal works anymore."

"You know that can be changed," Patricia said. "You've even seen how to do it, haven't you?"

"I know I can destroy it," I said.

"You can do more than that," Patricia said. "You're young yet."

"I'm older than you," I said.

"Young in your powers," she amended with a smile. "But I can help you. I can teach you so much more."

"Everyone wants to be my mentor," I grumbled. "Why does it feel like a trap?"

Patricia laughed. "With all due respect, you seem to be uniquely incapable of detecting when you're actually in a trap and when you're not."

I heard Sophie suck in a breath and looked away from Patricia's icy blue eyes to see several more witches in cloaks and hoods standing all around us, wands raised. I didn't take a head count, but I was pretty sure there were nine equally spaced around the perimeter of the tower's main floor. That plus Evanora and our mothers' old class-mates made thirteen.

"So you lured us into a trap," I said. "So we passed all your tests, apparently. What now? This is all too elaborate to be just another offer to be my mentor."

"But it is," Patricia said. "Well, it starts with that. I need to mentor you, but only until your power grows to be equal to mine."

"Why would you want that?" Brianna asked. "It sounds like it would be dangerous for you."

"I trust you," Patricia said. "I see your mother in you, and I always trusted her. She was my closest partner all through our school days. We drove each other to heights we'd never have reached alone. But she stepped away from magic, and now she's gone. I just want to have that same relationship again, with you."

"Why?" I asked.

"I miss it," she said. "You'll see what I mean when we start working together. There's nothing like it. But our kind of magic, time magic, it needs two witches. One witch alone can tweak at the threads that are already there. But to tap into the real power, the power to create new timelines, requires two witches working together. And there are so precious few of us around."

"That's what you want to do?" I asked. "Create a new timeline? Like, to get back to 1968?"

"That would just be the beginning," Patricia said.

"Don't listen to her, Amanda," Brianna said. "It has to be a trick."

"No trick," Patricia said, holding up her hands as if to show she wasn't hiding anything up her sleeves. "Why would I have to resort to tricks? To lie or deceive? I'm offering you a chance to master a skill of creation. Think of the possibilities."

"Juno told me that with her help I could undo death itself," I said.

"That's just one possibility," Patricia said. "Keep thinking. You'll come up with oh so many more."

"Why are there thirteen of you?" I asked. She blinked at this apparently out of nowhere question. "Thirteen, that's a number of power. Why amass all that power just to make me an offer you're sure I would never want to refuse? It seems so unnecessary."

"I confess, when it comes to magic, I like to think big," she said. She made a spokesmodel gesture to indicate the tower around us. "I had to get your attention and bring you here. Better too much than too little."

"It doesn't feel right," Sophie hissed at me through her teeth. I couldn't argue with that.

"You tested all three of us," I said, not really sure where I was going to end up, but I just had to think something through. Did they know how we flowed power through each other? How we were stronger together than just the sum of our parts?

I was willing to bet they didn't. I was willing to bet that wasn't how their particular coven worked.

"We did," Patricia said, still smiling at me.

"But you're only asking to mentor me," I said. "No mentors for Sophie or Brianna?"

"If it's important to you, I'm sure something could be arranged," Patricia said.

"But mine is the power you really need," I said.

"I don't want to take your power, Amanda," she said. "I just want the two of us to work together. To create things together."

"Sure," I said, not believing that was all of it. Not for a minute.

But she was never going to tell me what she really wanted. She wasn't going to let it slip. She had the upper hand, after all.

"If I stay, will you let the others go?" I asked.

"Amanda!" Brianna and Sophie said at once.

"No one is being held against their will here," Patricia said.

"Only there's no door," Otto said.

"Oh, silly me," Patricia said. "Linda can show you the door." Linda nodded and trotted past the three of us to where Otto and Edward were standing near the wall. Otto still had a firm hold on Edward's arm and shoulder and I wondered how many times he had had to restrain him while my back had been turned.

Linda swept her arms up over her head then brought them back down in a slow fanning motion, as if she were doing an interpretive dance about a rainbow. The wood-paneled wall shimmered then became a revolving door of glass with shining brass fixtures.

"You're not staying with them," Sophie said.

"I need you to get Edward and Otto out of here," I said.

"I don't believe for a moment that you're just buying us time," Sophie said. "I know that look in your eyes. I've seen it before. You want what she's offering you."

"You know it's a trap," Brianna said. "You know it."

"But what if it's possible to change things?" I asked. "What if we could go back to 1968 and see what really happened? What if we could change it? What if I could have a childhood with a mother who could actually talk to me?"

"Amanda," Sophie said. She sounded as if my words wounded her.

"I can fix things. I can fix everything," I said.

"Nothing is broken," Brianna said. "Time isn't broken. It just happened the way it happened."

"What a lovely argument against using magic from the one among us who uses it the most, and for the most mundane of purposes," Patricia said, looking around the room as if to see how many of the witches around us agreed with her.

"Amanda, we need to stick with our mission," Sophie said.

"Protect the time portal?" I asked.

"No," Sophie said. "That's Miss Zenobia's mission. I'm talking about our mission."

Her eyes were pleading with me to understand. She didn't want to spell it out with all of the other witches around us, listening in.

But we didn't know anything they didn't already know. We knew far less, if truth be told. The blonde girl in front of me knew far more about my own mother than I ever would.

Our mothers. That was the mission Sophie was talking about. Patricia and her friends knew exactly what happened that day in 1968 and in the days after. But would they tell us the truth?

And how would I be able to tell if anything they said was the truth or not? My eyes shifted from Patricia to Debra. She was the one who had taken our memories, who had wiped the memories of every police officer who had known about the wardrobe and the murder victim from the wrong time. What more could she do?

"You knew my mother better than I ever will," I said to Patricia, who looked saddened by my words.

"I'll tell you all about her, I promise," Patricia said. "She was my closest friend."

"Maybe she was, once," I said. "But for some reason, she turned on you, didn't she? And I don't know why. Maybe I never will. But I know she did. And you know what? That's good enough for me."

Then I blinked into the world of webs and I started pulling threads.

CHAPTER 20

*M*y triumphant moment was cut abruptly short. I was not alone. And Patricia, despite being younger than me, had spent a lot more years studying magic. The moment I sensed her before me, I knew she knew things about the web of threads I had yet to discover.

Because while I knew she was there, I couldn't see her. I only saw the effect she was having on the threads around her. And I was pretty sure I only saw that because she wanted me to.

I stayed near my physical form, nervous that she could do something to the connection I shared with it here, but also that something might happen to it back inside the tower. I tried to think of something else I could do, some way I could shield myself then carry on fighting.

Too late, I realized that Patricia's warping of the threads wasn't random, and it wasn't some way of drawing in power that I didn't recognize. She was weaving, making new nodes between threads around me, then drawing them tight.

She was catching me in a net, and it was closing in around me. I tried to move the threads, but they didn't respond to me. I was trapped.

And then she started cutting. I had been worried she might sever the connection I had to my own body, but she wasn't.

She was cutting me away from the entire world.

The net tightened further, the threads biting into me despite neither of us having a physical form in that world. More tightening, more burning. I did the only thing I had left to do.

I went back into my own body.

But the world around me was in chaos. There was a loud cracking noise and flashes of strobing light, over and over, and I was pretty sure if I hadn't already fallen to the ground I'd be in danger of having my hair catch on fire.

Evanora was yelling something, but I couldn't make out the words over the popping sound.

Then I felt the net tightening again, invisible lashes burning into my flash. I cried out.

The popping suddenly stopped, and I could hear Evanora still yelling, "it's only fireworks!"

Then Edward was at my side, trying to help me up, but my body was writhing.

"Amanda!" he said, panic in his voice.

"Patricia!" I said, or tried to. I don't think I got all the sounds out. But he looked up and saw Patricia hovering over us, arms out, pointed toes several feet above the soot-stained marble floor. Her eyes were rolled back, so nothing showed but the whites, and I was sure she was still in the world of webs.

As if she heard my thoughts she tightened the net again, and my vision started to darken.

I was losing my place in the world.

"We have to get out of here!" Sophie yelled. She and Brianna were standing back to back hurling spells at the witches that circled around us like a hurricane of cloaks and hoods. "Can you carry her?"

"Yes!" Edward said, but rather than bending to pick me up he got to his feet. I heard a hiss and then saw him throw another string of firecrackers straight at Patricia's head. She screamed and fell to the floor, pulled nastily back into the real world.

But my body was still trembling, as weak and incapable of responding to my commands as a newborn's.

Edward threw me over his shoulder and ran to where Sophie and Brianna were backing towards the door. I couldn't see much past the back of Edward's coat, and what I could see was upside-down and tended to spin for no reason. But I was pretty sure I wasn't seeing Otto because he wasn't there.

"Hurry!" Brianna yelled. "She's closing it!"

"No, she isn't," Sophie growled. I heard a smack like someone taking a punch followed by a yelp of pain. Then Edward was running again. My head lolled back and forth, but out of the corner of my eye, I just caught the sight of Linda on the floor, trying with both hands to contain a vigorously bleeding nose.

Then we were back out in the darkness. Even in the dead of winter, the smell of spoiled garbage and old urine was strong.

"Otto?" Brianna said.

"There," Sophie said, and we were running again, out of the court-yard. I could hear the sound of an engine roaring and of metal scraping on brick, then a squeal of tires on a road.

"Come on!" Otto yelled, and I was watching the alley rush past me. We reached the car and Edward dumped me into the center of the back seat, he and Brianna piling in on either side of me. Sophie slid in the passenger-side window but remained sitting on the door frame rather than getting into the car.

"Amanda?" Brianna said, taking my head into her hands to look into my eyes. I couldn't make my mouth work. "What did she do to you?"

"Is she going to be all right?" Edward asked. The fear in his voice broke my heart.

I couldn't even blink my eyes, but I didn't need to. My conscious-ness really wanted to be in that other world. For a moment I was afraid if I went there, I'd never be able to come back. But I had no choice.

I kept myself anchored close to my body, not sure what would happen when Otto slammed on the accelerator. I anchored myself to threads from the car itself just to be sure. Then I took my first close look at my own self. Not my physical body, which seemed unharmed despite all of the pain I had been feeling. My actual self.

It's hard to explain. There was nothing to see, not visually. And it took a bit of work to really be aware of myself. When I finally got it in focus, it was all I could do not to cry.

I was in tatters. Threads were torn or snipped and left dangling. Delicate intersections had become knots pulled too tight.

But I knew how to fix it. The minute I thought about what I should do, I was instantly sure it was the right thing.

Briefly, I remembered that Sophie thought this knowledge came from somewhere, from some entity not to be trusted. But in that moment, I had no other choice.

I repaired myself. I loosened the knots so that they functioned as a meeting of threads with give and take again. Then I fixed the broken threads themselves. Nothing so inelegant as tying the torn ends back together. No, it was more like I could create a new thread by rolling the cut threads together. When I was done, it was like they'd never been snipped at all.

I came to in the car and sucked in a deep breath of air.

"She's back!" Edward said. He was leaning over me with tears in his eyes but a big grin on his face. "You stopped breathing. How are you now?"

"Good," I croaked, then rolled my head to look at Brianna, but she wasn't there.

Or rather, she wasn't sitting on the back seat next to me. Now she was sitting like Sophie, her entire top half out the window.

"What's going on?" I asked.

"They're chasing us," he said.

Otto swore and spun the steering wheel, turning the car without slowing down. I felt the left side of the car lifting off the ground. Edward grabbed onto the window frame to keep from crushing me, but I was sliding away from him.

We were going to roll over. I could feel it.

Then something banged on the roof, and we slammed back down onto four wheels.

"How are they chasing us?" I asked, sitting up and turning to look out the back window. My whole body hurt, but at least I could move it around. I'm not sure I ever appreciated that fact enough before.

"They've got cars," Edward said.

I counted three cars behind us, weaving from one side of the road to the other, occasionally dodging some other unfortunate soul out driving the residential streets of St. Paul late on a Sunday night. I couldn't tell one witch from another in the darkness, but I could see the flash from their wands. Then we passed under a streetlight that lit up their faces for the briefest of moments.

They were hanging out the windows like Sophie and Brianna. They were also standing on the running boards. One was even sitting cross-legged on the roof of one of the cars.

"I can't outrun them," Otto said, shouting so that Sophie and Brianna could hear him.

"I can lose them," Sophie shouted back. I couldn't see what she was doing, but I could guess, especially when the cold February night air that was blasting through all the open windows became a gentle breeze. Warm. Smelling of beignets, coffee, jasmine, and something else.

Ah, Antoine. I had never noticed that undertone in her magic wind before. But that was definitely his own unique smell.

"Turn again," Sophie said. "Slower this time. No hurry."

Otto grumbled under his breath, but when he turned down a side street, we were only briefly on two wheels and required no magical intervention to keep from rolling over.

I looked out the back window again and watched the three cars continue down the road we had abandoned.

"Hiding from witches," Sophie said as she slid into her seat and rolled up her window. "The very first thing I learned how to do and the most important."

"I'm not sure you bought us all that much time," Otto said. "They know where you're going."

"It'll be enough," Brianna said as she too got back inside the car and shut the window.

"Enough time for what?" Edward asked.

"To get away. To get back home," she said.

"But where's home?" he asked.

Brianna looked at me, leaving that answer up to me.

"A different time," I said. "A different world. You know we don't really belong here."

"But you'll be back," he said, not quite putting a question mark on the end of that.

But we were already at the school. Otto slammed on the brakes and bumped up against the curb. Brianna and Sophie had their doors open even before the car came to a stop, but Edward grabbed my arm, not letting me follow them out of the car.

"I don't know," I said. "But I swear, if it's at all possible, I will."

"But how will I know?" he asked. "I either see you or I don't? Forever?"

"I'll find a way to get word to you. But you have to let me go."

He looked down at his own hand as if not realizing he had been detaining me and quickly let me go.

"They're here," Otto said. "Go, quickly!"

But I needed to do something first. Even though I didn't have enough time to do it properly, I kissed Edward good-bye.

I looked into his eyes for what I was really afraid was going to be the very last time.

And I ran to join Sophie and Brianna at the edge of the time portal.

CHAPTER 21

"*D*o we have a plan?" Sophie asked as we stood together under the fruit trees. Without any of us making a conscious choice to do it, we had gotten into our usual formation.

"Yes," I said, hoping they didn't notice that the hand I used to push back my hair was trembling like mad. "I just need you two to channel power into me. I can take it from there."

"Is that going to be enough?" Sophie asked. "There are thirteen of them and only three of us."

"But the difference is, they don't work together," I said. "Not like we do. They can't help each other or flow energy between each other like we do. We've got this."

"What if we don't even need to fight them?" Brianna asked.

"What do you mean?" I asked.

"Let's go into the time portal. We can stand on the bridge and hold that position. We don't know they can even get that far, do we?" she asked.

"Patricia can," I said.

"But will she, though?" Sophie asked. "I'm with Brianna. Let's not face them here."

I wasn't so sure that was a good idea. Just the thought of facing

Patricia again in the world of threads made my blood run cold. But I couldn't tell them that. Even if I had the time to describe it right, what would be the point in making them afraid before the fight even started?

"Let's go," I said, lifting my arms.

We had never done this before, just lingered between 1928 and 2019. I could sense both worlds. I could feel how 2019 was ever so slightly colder. How the school in 1928 was filled with people while in 2019 it was just Mr. Trevor.

I could sense Otto and Edward. They hadn't fled. They were in Coco's yard, looking for a place where they could see into the charm school backyard.

They weren't making it easy to keep them safe.

Then the witches were there, flowing around both sides of the house to spread out across the backyard.

The three of us couldn't speak, but we could sense each other's thoughts. Not in words, more like in the raw idea form.

Brianna was focused on the wards. We had been bolstering and strengthening the ones Miss Zenobia had left behind for months, and adding several new ones. That investment over time was going to aid us now. She was pleased the effort had been worth it.

Sophie was noting what I had suspected, that none of the coven witches seemed to even sense the portal, let alone have access to it.

None, that is, until Patricia arrived.

She advanced on the fruit orchard, looking straight at the point where the time bridge touched the ground, and without even slowing her step, she started pulling at threads, unraveling months of our careful work.

The wards around us were popping like those firecrackers had before.

I caught onto the threads that formed the bridge and began reinforcing them. Patricia was still going after the wards, but we could always redo those later. Without the bridge itself, we'd be cut off from 1928.

Sophie and Brianna sensed I was using my magic and immediately began channeling energy into me. I could feel Brianna's despair at the loss of the wards, but she was keeping a restraint on it. Nothing like the torrent of thought she'd hit me with before.

By the time the last ward fell, I had the bridge itself so full of power it was glowing.

I was also sinking into it. I hadn't intended to do that, but it felt like the right thing to do. The bridge bound with me would be stronger.

Patricia paused to reassess now that the wards were gone. I could feel her sensing me, probing at me. Angry, I thrust back at her.

I didn't really know what I was doing. It felt like something burst, and suddenly I was overrun with images. Thoughts. Feelings.

Memories.

I saw my mother. I saw all of our mothers, and Patricia and Linda and Debra too. I saw them all fighting.

But it was a jumble that made little sense and disappeared from my mind as quickly as it had appeared.

I could tell that the fact it had happened at all was making Patricia very angry indeed. Someone had let her down. That was the feeling I was getting. That feeling of something bursting, was that me breaking into her mind, or a walled-off section of her mind suddenly breaking open?

It really felt like the second thing.

Her anger was pulsing darkly, warping the threads around her as if they wanted to escape her presence. Then she turned her attention to the bridge, pulling threads by the fistful and trying to tear them to shreds.

They held fast, but the effort was draining me faster than Sophie and Brianna could feed me more power.

And yet I could see the effort was draining Patricia as well.

The question was, which of us was going to collapse first?

I was determined that it wouldn't be me. I put all my focus into just holding the bridge together.

Then I got a tiny bit of thought from Brianna. A little sliver of that memory blast I had just triggered. Apparently it had washed over her and Sophie as well, but Brianna being Brianna, she had held onto at least a part of it.

She was showing us a fragment of a memory, of our mothers working together. Like us, they were fighting Patricia on her own. And like now the fight was on the bridge between times.

But unlike us, they weren't trying to hold the bridge together. They were the ones trying to destroy it.

Why?

Sophie was thinking the same question.

But Brianna was thinking something else. She was thinking maybe we should be doing the same thing. Destroy the bridge, trap Patricia in 1928 and we could rest easy in the present.

I didn't like it. It was exactly the opposite of what Miss Zenobia had asked us to do.

There had to be a reason that Miss Zenobia had told us that the bridge couldn't be destroyed, when I had realized from the first moment I had my power that that simply wasn't true.

But there also had to be a reason our mothers had attempted to do just that.

I wasn't sure if that was my thought or Brianna's. Maybe it didn't matter anymore.

Patricia's energy was flagging, her attack slowing. I felt like I was moving through rapidly drying cement myself, clumsily catching hold of threads before they slipped away from me. Holding it all together.

I was certain that destroying the bridge was the wrong choice. And yet, I was equally certain that whatever reason our mothers had had for what they tried to do, they hadn't been wrong.

They certainly hadn't meant to *do* wrong.

Patricia was still chipping away at the bridge, and I knew even if she fell away in exhaustion, the moment she had recovered, she would be back.

Unless she couldn't find the bridge again.

All at once, the three of us saw what we had to do. We moved as one, all three of us part of the bridge now. We stretched, longer and longer, extending the bridge like we were rolling a bit of dough into the thinnest possible rope.

Then thinner and then thinner still.

I'm not sure at what point Patricia fell away. I could just barely sense her lying on the snow under the trees in 1928. Cursing our names.

Sophie and Brianna tried to stop then, but I kept going. Maybe Brianna understood what I was doing better than I did, but it felt like I was trying to make a tunnel through time rather than a bridge. And this tunnel would be so narrow only something the size of a bacterium could squeeze through it.

Certainly not a witch.

Brianna thought the word "wormhole" at me. I guess that might be what we were making. Only in movies those were how starships got around, and in this case nothing was ever meant to pass through it.

It was a compromise. The bridge was effectively destroyed. And yet the essence of it was still there.

The moment I stopped working the tube ever smaller, I heard a sound. I think it was Juno crying out, but whether in pain or alarm or something else, I don't know.

Then we were under the trees, each of us collapsed on the snow, completely spent.

I didn't even try to get up. I just closed my eyes and let the darkness take me.

CHAPTER 22

*T*he three of us spent the better part of a week mostly sleeping. Partly this was because we were exhausted. We had never done that much magical work before. And partly this was because we just could. With the time portal shrunken down to almost nothing, there was no reason to do more than verify the few wards we had cast over it were still there and check Brianna's detecting equipment for any other sign of change. Our morning ritual was no longer necessary.

But mostly it was because, in that moment, the work we needed to do had to be done sleeping.

Brianna had crafted a special bedtime tea, which we all drank early in the evening. It was nasty, like drinking the runoff from a flooded graveyard, muddy and putrid. It took a lot of honey to get it down. A lot of honey.

It was meant to give us lucid dreams, dreams where we would know we were dreaming and could steer the events. In the dreams, we had access to memories. We could steer our dreams away from skating penguins and keep them focused on the past. We could relive those moments and remember it all with complete clarity when we woke.

I relived my childhood from my very first memory of a goat peeing on me when I tried to pet it at the county fair to the last moment I spent with my mother, watching the life go out of her eyes.

I remembered nothing useful. My mother had never given me any hint of her past at all, and if she had been afraid of that past catching up with her, she had never shown it.

The three of us also tried to recapture that burst of memory we had gotten from Patricia during the fight on the time bridge, but none of us could summon up more than a few fragmentary images.

By the end of the week, we all agreed. What we needed to know wasn't hiding from us inside our own heads.

"So what do we do now?" Sophie said as we all sat in the library comparing notes. Brianna had succeeded in turning both Sophie and me into obsessive journal-keepers. What had started as a way of recording what we had dreamed the moment we woke up was becoming a growing addiction to write down any thought any time it struck.

"Could we get back to 1928 if we needed to?" I asked. "That's my main worry."

"Why would we need to?" Brianna asked.

"We left a lot of people potentially in danger," I said.

"Otto will look after Edward," Sophie said. "They're both young and unattached. They could blow town and start a new life in a different state or even country if they had to."

"And the school is safe," Brianna said. "We warded it well. And Miss Zenobia is still there."

"Doesn't it seem strange to you that we can't see her when she's there?" I asked. "Surely it's within her power."

"Maybe it is, and she chooses not to," Sophie said. "For her own reasons."

"Like she's hiding from us," I said.

"If we have to we can expand the portal back to the way it was," Brianna said. "We didn't destroy it. We just changed its form."

"It's probably safer for the others if we stay in our own time," Sophie said.

"I feel like we're surrounded by potential time bombs," I said. "There are all sorts of things they can do to attack us, but we can't get at them."

"Time is an arrow," Brianna said, but mostly to herself.

"None of us had anything useful in the memories that they stole," I said. "So, what does that mean? Was Patricia being honest when she said it was just to get our attention?"

"There are a lot more direct ways to get our attention," Sophie said.

I got up from the table and walked over to the chalkboard. We hadn't discovered any of the others' names. Brianna and Sophie had made some guesses about some of the powers the others had from the spells they had deflected during the car chase, but because the witches had all been cloaked and hooded, we didn't know who had which power.

There was so much we didn't know.

"Patricia lies," I decided. "There was a reason they went through all of that trouble instead of just sending us a letter or something."

"They would've had to prepare," Brianna said. "And they would've had to wait in that state of preparedness until Miss Zenobia was gone and they were confident of how long she'd be away."

"So they started planning after New Year's Eve?" Sophie asked.

"Maybe sooner, but definitely by then," Brianna said. "Two months of waiting. Miss Zenobia must have gone into the time portal, because she certainly didn't leave the city or even the house."

"Were the students still in the school, do you think?" I asked.

"I think so," Brianna said, paging through her notes. "A lot of the spells we undid were specifically to cloak them. One thing we know for sure is that Linda was a master of glamour. She hid an entire skyscraper from us, inside and out. She hid it from everybody."

"How did they even build the thing?" Sophie said. "Maybe it wasn't real. Maybe it was just an illusion."

"It looked real," I said. "It felt real. But the warehouse did too. I touched that tile covered in layers of dust, and I touched that marble floor. I could feel the texture. They were both completely real."

"Debra seems equally powerful with memory," Sophie said. "For all we know, we can't remember anything helpful because we only *thought* we got our real memories back. Maybe she just put another spell in our heads to make us remember false memories."

"Oh, don't say that," I said, clutching at my head. "I don't want to be constantly questioning everything."

"How can you not?" Sophie asked.

"That's the problem," I sighed. "I already was. But don't rub it in."

"While it's certainly true that she could put such a spell on us and even make us forget she had ever done it, I don't think that's the case," Brianna said. "She didn't have the opportunity during the fight, and none of them can pull another heist inside the charm school. I promise you the wards will keep them out now."

"I hope you're right," I said. "But I can't help remembering how badly we got tricked. We were right in their lair the entire time, and none of us had a clue."

"That eats at me too," Sophie said.

"I know I could've seen it if I had gone to the world of threads," I said. "But I didn't. Not even once. And I don't know why I didn't."

"It wasn't part of the plan," Brianna said. "That's all."

"But how do I know I never did because some sort of hypnotic suggestion hiding in my mind was telling me not to? I didn't hear it like a voice in my head, but I obeyed it all the same."

"Now you're making *me* paranoid," Sophie said.

"I don't think so," Brianna said.

"But doesn't it make sense that they would do that? To keep me from realizing we were walking into a trap?"

"No," Brianna said, "because the whole point of that trap had been to make you do just that. To go to the world of webs and unleash your power. That's what Patricia wanted. All of that talk about the two of you working together, I think that was all a ruse."

"But time magic does take two witches, doesn't it?" Sophie asked.

"For the complicated stuff, yeah," Brianna said. "But think about it. The moment Amanda reached for that power, Patricia immediately started cutting her off from the world. I think that was her plan all along."

"She didn't try talking to me there," I said. "She just jumped me."

"But why?" Sophie said. "You're saying she and the others stole our memories, lured us into the past and into a trap, all just to cut Amanda out of the world? Why? Does she blame you for something your mother did?"

"I wish I knew," I said.

"Maybe one or all of us does have a memory they don't want us to have, we just don't recognize its significance," Brianna said. "If we could dig up other clues, it might trigger something."

"But dig up clues where?" Sophie said, lifting her hands to indicate the library and house around us. "We've looked everywhere."

"No, we haven't," I said. "Not remotely. We've only searched this one place. Maybe it's time to expand that."

"What are you talking about? We can't leave," Sophie said.

"Can't we? We no longer need the ritual to watch the time portal. It doesn't take three of us to just check on things every so often," I said.

"But where would we go?" Brianna asked. "This is where our mothers last were before they disappeared. Where else could there be clues?"

"Where they died," I said. "Not mine. My mother never did magic after I was born. But your mothers met with other witches. Those witches might know something."

"I can call Sephora and talk to her," Brianna said.

"You could, but I think you'll find out more if you actually go to Boston. Talk to everybody. Get your mother's full story. Ask every witch what she knows about Miss Zenobia, even if it's all rumor or innuendo."

"You want to investigate Miss Zenobia?" Brianna asked.

"No, that makes sense, Bree," Sophie said. "I agree with Amanda. It feels like she held out on us. She didn't tell us the whole story about the time portal and what happened with her sister. And I really think she could see us and talk to us in 1928 if she wanted to. There must be a reason she doesn't."

"It feels wrong leaving the two of you here. I'm sure Sephora would be willing to ask any questions of anyone we think might know something," Brianna said.

"Sophie is going too," I said. "Not to Boston, but back to New Orleans."

Sophie nodded as if she had known I would say that. "It's time to find out what really happened to my mother. Now that I have real magic to help me."

"I'll stay here," I said. "There's nothing useful back in Scandia, and Nick is looking into the official missing persons reports and anything else he can find through his channels. I should be around in case he turns up anything."

"Splitting up doesn't feel like the right thing to do," Brianna said, hugging herself as if the thought made her suddenly cold.

"It's only for a few days," I said. "Long enough to find out all you can. And we'll be in contact the entire time."

"And you'll summon us back here the minute there's even a hint of trouble," Sophie said. "You won't try to face down a threat alone."

"I promise to call for help if I need it," I said. "I'm not going to risk everything thinking I can handle it on my own. If a mouse slides through that time portal, I'll be waiting for you to get here before I touch it."

"Then I guess we should start making some travel arrangements," Brianna said.

"At least there's one good thing," Sophie said.

"Going home again?" I asked.

"No, I was thinking that at least tonight we don't have to choke down any of that tea," Sophie said.

CHAPTER 23

*M*iss Zenobia Weekes had built a pretty massive house all for the purpose of keeping a watch over the time portal in the back garden. I suppose she had to. There were no small houses on Summit Avenue. Most of them were proper mansions, especially on the side that overlooked the river valley.

I don't know if making the house into a school had been part of the plan from the start, the presence of students being part of the camouflage or what. Maybe in all of those decades she spent trying to reach her sister, she had just gotten lonely.

Whatever the reason, the house was huge. I could spend entire days moving from room to room going about my own business and never bumping into either Sophie or Brianna or Mr. Trevor.

But I would know they were there. I would hear the sounds of pages turning in the library and the scribble of a pen on paper. Sophie was light as air when she danced, but the touch of her toes on the attic floor was still a familiar cadence. Even Mr. Trevor coughed or sneezed from time to time.

It had only been an hour since Mr. Trevor had loaded Brianna and Sophie's bags into the trunk of the town car and driven them to the airport, but I was already going mad from the silence. Even the cats, apparently feeling betrayed by Brianna's departure, had disappeared into the walls or wherever it was that cats went when you couldn't find them anywhere.

I found myself in the kitchen making another cup of tea I didn't even really want. I just couldn't stand being so aware that I was the only one breathing inside that enormous house. The soft roar of the electric kettle helped.

I was just pouring the water into the mug when Mr. Trevor came in the back door.

"Do you want some tea, Mr. Trevor?" I offered.

"Tea would be lovely," he said as he came into the kitchen tugging off his gloves. "Everyone is off safe and sound. I checked their flight information on my phone after I parked the car."

"This house gets so quiet when no one is here," I said. "How did you stand it all those months alone?"

"Well, Cynthia had been here with me during the day," he said. "The nights could be long at times."

"What was Miss Zenobia like?" I asked. "You knew her better than anybody, right?"

"I don't know if that's strictly speaking true," he said. "She was so often away."

"I got the sense from her journal that that became necessary after our mothers left the school in 1968," I said.

"Yes, a bit before my time," he said, bending to blow on his tea. "I've often wondered what this place was like when it was an active school. Perhaps a bit crowded. That's strange to think about."

"Did she ever talk to you about her sister?" I asked.

"She never mentioned her at all," he said. "I didn't even know she had one until you told me about her."

"And yet everything she did was because of her sister," I said. "It must've been lonely, keeping what was most important to her a secret."

"Oh, yes. She was very lonely," he said. "Cynthia and I tried our best to be companions to her. But I'm sure we were poor substitutes."

"For her sister?" I asked.

"Maybe not specifically," he said. "She was centuries old with a power I can scarcely imagine, and a responsibility I can't even grasp. And she had no one to shoulder any of that burden with her. Yes, I think she was very lonely."

"She could've gone back east to where there were other old, powerful witches," I said. "Or she could've invited one to come here and stay with her. Didn't she have any friends?"

"She never spoke of other witches to me," Mr. Trevor said. "Perhaps her journal could tell you more."

"Maybe," I said. Brianna had explained how to decode it and left me with all of her notes and a fresh notebook to transcribe into, but I really wasn't looking forward to starting that task.

"She was a very private person," Mr. Trevor said. "And neither Cynthia nor I were the type to pry. But we both knew she was sad. She was always tired. Her work was very draining, and she did it all alone. She was lonely. But she never wavered."

"She was driven? Determined?" I asked.

"No, it was more like regret," he said. "She had so many regrets, and her strongest motivation was not to add to them."

"I wish she would've found us before she died," I said. "I wish we could've had more time to learn from her and hear all of her stories."

Mr. Trevor gave me a sad smile as he picked up his tea to head upstairs. "I believe that too was one of her regrets," he said.

I made as much noise as I could filling the cats' bowls with kibble, but none of them came running.

Perhaps they just needed more time. They liked me well enough as a substitute for Brianna when she was too busy rushing around the library to give pets.

I spent the rest of the afternoon and all of the evening after dinner working on decoding the journal. It was slow work, first decoding the words and then translating them into English and then trying to figure out which of those two steps had gone wrong when the result didn't make sense.

When I finally went up to bed I found that I couldn't fall asleep. I had had the same trouble the night before, and Brianna thought it might be withdrawal from her dream tea. I smiled as I remembered the look on Sophie's face when she discovered that Brianna had exposed us both to an addictive substance without warning us first.

I was just drifting off when something hopped lightly onto the bed beside me, kneaded at the comforter tucked behind my knees, then settled into a tight, purring ball. A few minutes later I had two more purring balls of fur snuggling against me. The sound of their purring and breathing was better than a lullaby.

I didn't wake up until nearly midmorning, but I knew what I had to do.

I threw off the covers and ran up to the attic to get dressed in the clothes from my wardrobe up there. The one that held all of my 1920s clothes. I had my wand, Cynthia's amulet, and the cloak enchanted with all of Brianna's cloaking spells.

Long before I knew I was a witch and had the power to see time and read people's stories in the threads that connected them to all of the world around them, I had known I had something about me that made me different from other people. I couldn't see the future, and I had never considered it any sort of luck, but sometimes I would just know I had to do something, or to avoid some other thing. I had relied on it. It had never steered me wrong.

But when I went out to the orchard on my own and reached out with my power to find the end of the time portal, it wasn't that sort of feeling that was guiding me.

I knew I was doing the right thing. I had complete confidence in that. Not just that it was a thing I ought to do, but that it was a thing I *could* do.

I knew I could use my power to pass through that portal, narrow as it was. I could arrange my own threads end to end in one long string that was fine enough to pass through the eye of the needle that was all that was left of the gate to the time portal.

It wasn't a compulsion, like those feelings from before. Those had descended on me as if from on high, and I had obeyed their demands.

This wasn't that. This was a choice. But I knew in my bones it was the right one.

I reassembled myself in the 1928 version of the orchard, touched Cynthia's amulet I wore around my neck and then the wand tucked away in its hidden pocket. Like the cloak, they were still with me.

But I didn't expand my awareness to look for the other witches. If they were watching then they already knew I was there. They weren't going to stop me.

I followed the path around the side of the house to the sidewalk, then followed Summit Avenue until I reached the cobblestoned side street lined with carriage houses that was Maiden's Way.

I didn't know what day of the week it was; I had lost track during the week of sleeping. I didn't know what time it was, except too late for breakfast but too early for lunch.

But I knew as I climbed the narrow staircase to the apartment over one of those carriage houses that when I knocked on that door, Edward would answer.

And he did. He was dressed for work but still home, and he flung open the door at the first touch of my knuckles as if he had been waiting for me the whole time.

"Amanda!" he said. "What are you doing here? Is it safe? Is it all over?"

"It might never be all over," I said.

"Then why are you here?"

"Because this is where I'm supposed to be," I said, but then shook my head. "No. It's where I *want* to be."

He started to smile at that, but the worried line between his eyebrows quickly reasserted itself. "But the witches-"

"Aren't going to stop me," I said.

"Stop you from doing what?" he asked.

My best smile just seemed to confuse him, but that's OK. When I grabbed hold of the front of his jacket and tugged him down to meet my kiss, that confusion was gone.

He kissed me back, with gusto. But then he pulled away from me again to look me in the eye.

"Otto told me where you're from," he said. "Is it true?"

"Yes," I said.

"So this, us, is going to be complicated," he said.

"Yes."

"It might not last," he said.

I really, really, really wanted to lie to him. But I couldn't. "Anytime we're apart, there's a good chance I won't be able to get back to you again. It can happen at any time, without warning."

"And you're okay with that?" he asked.

"Are you?"

"Well, that's true of anyone, isn't it?" he said. "I could get hit by a bus tomorrow, and you'd never see me again."

"This is different," I said.

"Maybe it's better," he said. "Every minute is precious, and we can never forget that. We'll always be living every moment together as if it could be the last. Even if those moments end up being all too few, they'll be so much richer."

"You think so?" I asked.

"I know so," he said. "Here, I'll show you right now."

Then he picked me up, spinning me around and into his little apartment, and kicking the door shut behind us.

Oh, how he showed me.

CHECK OUT BOOK SIX!

The Witches Three will return in Charm Offensive, out now!

The Witches Three agreed to split up to better investigate their mother's pasts. Brianna lurks deep in the witchiest parts of Boston, researching in secret libraries and questioning covens that date back further than the English colonies. Sophie stalks mysterious wielders of magic through parts of the French Quarter of New Orleans that tourists never see.

And Amanda, alone in Miss Zenobia Weekes' Charm School for Exceptional Young Ladies, breaks all the rules. She juggles her time between 2019, coordinating the investigation with the other two, and 1928, where Edward awaits her. She knows she can't go on living two lives forever. Always she expects the 1928 coven to ambush her.

To her surprise, the attack comes in 2019, when her good friend Nick disappears. Not like a missing person, but like he never existed. His own grandfather doesn't recognize his name or photo.

Investigating murders? Old hat for the Witches Three. But investigating a person who never existed? Could be tricky.

Charm Offensive, Book 6 in the Witches Three Cozy Mystery series!

CHECK OUT THE FIRST BOOK IN A
BRAND NEW SERIES!

The Viking Witch Cozy Mystery Series starts here with Body at the Crossroads.

When her mother dies after a long illness, Ingrid Torfa must sell the family home to cover the medical bills. Her career as a book illustrator not yet exactly launched, Ingrid faces two options: live in her battered old Volkswagen, or go back to her mother's small town in northern Minnesota.

The small town that still haunts her dreams more than a decade since she last visited it. Or rather, not the town but the grandmother.

All of the drawings she fills notebooks with witches and the trolls that do their bidding? Not as whimsical in her nightmares as she sketches them in the bright light of day.

If not for her beloved cat Mjolner, living in the Volkswagen just might tempt her.

But the cat wants four walls and a door, so north she goes. And finds trouble in the form of a dead body before she even finds her grandmother's little town. How much can a town of stoic fishermen possibly be hiding?

As Ingrid is about to find out, quite a lot.

Body at the Crossroads, the first book in the Viking Witch Cozy Mystery series!

ALSO FROM RATATOSKR PRESS

The Ritchie and Fitz Sci-Fi Murder Mysteries starts with Murder on the Intergalactic Railway.

For Murdina Ritchie, acceptance at the Oymyakon Foreign Service Academy means one last chance at her dream of becoming a diplomat for the Union of Free Worlds. For Shackleton Fitz IV, it represents his last chance not to fail out of military service entirely.

Strange that fate should throw them together now, among the last group of students admitted after the start of the semester. They had once shared the strongest of friendships. But that all ended a long time ago.

But when an insufferable but politically important woman turns up murdered, the two agree to put their differences aside and work together to solve the case.

Because the murderer might strike again. But more importantly, solving a murder would just have to impress the dour colonel who clearly thinks neither of them belong at his academy.

Murder on the Intergalactic Railway, the first book in the Ritchie and Fitz Sci-Fi Murder Mysteries.

FREE EBOOK!

Like exclusive, free content?

If you'd like to receive "Enter Three Witches", a free trilogy of short stories, prequel to the Witches Three Cozy Mystery series, go to CateMartin.com to subscribe to my monthly newsletter! This eBook is exclusively for newsletter subscribers. Check it out!

ABOUT THE AUTHOR

Cate Martin is a mystery writer who lives in Minneapolis, Minnesota.

ALSO BY CATE MARTIN

The Witches Three Cozy Mystery Series

Charm School

Work Like a Charm

Third Time is a Charm

Old World Charm

Charm his Pants Off

Charm Offensive

The Viking Witch Cozy Mystery Series

Body at the Crossroads

Death Under the Bridge

Murder on the Lake

Killing in the Village Commons

Bloodshed in the Forest

Corpse in the Mead Hall